He eyed her as a falcon would its prey

"I'm tired, and I should like to go to bed," Danielle said coldly.

"So should I, *mignonne*. I shall escort you myself...I had not realized my new bride would be so anxious to consummate the vows we'd just made. I find your eagerness refreshing."

Jourdan was smiling, amusement lighting the depths of his eyes, but Danielle was white and rigid with shock, her eyes enormous in her small pale face.

"You can't mean it," she stammered wildly. "You don't want me.... It was just to get the oil company—"

"Which I have and intend to keep," Jourdan cut in icily, his laughter banished. "You are my wife, Danielle, and by the time dawn pearls the morning sky you will be so in deed, as well as in word."

PENNY JORDAN

JORDAN

daughter of hassan

Harlequin Books

TORONTO • NEW YORK • LOS ANGELES • LONDON
AMSTERDAM • PARIS • SYDNEY • HAMBURG
STOCKHOLM • ATHENS • TOKYO • MILAN

Harlequin Presents first edition October 1982
ISBN 0-373-10537-1

Original hardcover edition published in 1982
by Mills & Boon Limited

CHAPTER ONE

'DADDY, it's gorgeous, but you really shouldn't spoil me like this,' Danielle protested, eyeing her tall bearded stepfather in his flowing Arab robes.

'Nonsense,' he protested firmly, taking the diamond pendant from her and securing it round her slender throat. 'You might not be my daughter by blood and birth, Danielle, but you are still the child of my heart, and it pleases me greatly to "spoil" you, as you term it—although what spoiling this simple trinket could achieve, I really do not know,' he concluded with a smile. 'If I had my way your present would have been something far more fitting—emeralds to match your eyes; pearls from the Gulf to complement the creamy pallor of your skin.'

Danielle laughed, knowing when she was beaten. Her own father had died before she was born, and when she was thirteen her mother had met and married Sheikh Hassan Ibn Ahmed, head of a huge oil empire, whom she had met at a reception given by its British equivalent, for whom she worked.

Danielle and her stepfather had hit it off right away. Although previously married, the Sheikh had no children from that marriage. His first wife had divorced him, and although nothing had been said, Danielle guessed that he was perhaps unable to father children of his own, which made his great love for her all the more poignant.

Although he lived and worked in London,

running the huge multi-million-pound oil empire, the oil which fuelled this empire came from the tiny state ruled by his elder brother, sandwiched tightly between Kuwait and Saudi Arabia.

Although nothing had ever been said, Danielle had the impression that her stepfather's family did not approve of his marriage. Perhaps that was why none of them had ever visited them in the elegant St. John's Wood apartment which was their London home, or the country estate in Dorset close to where Danielle had gone to school.

However, whatever they thought of Sheikh Hassan's marriage, it was plain that his financial and business acumen was highly regarded, for otherwise Danielle knew that they would never have trusted him to have what amounted to the sole responsibility for their far-reaching business activities.

Occasionally some of his countrymen did visit their home, but Danielle rarely saw them. For one thing it was only two years since she had left her Swiss finishing school, and for another, Hassan preferred not to involve his wife and stepdaughter in his business affairs.

In fact it was because of this that they had come close to having their first quarrel, for which the diamond pendant had been a peace-offering, Danielle suspected.

Following her year at finishing school she had returned to England determined to find herself a job, but her stepfather had been horrified. There was no need for her to work; did she want to shame him by implying that he could not afford to support her?

Danielle had called on her mother to intervene

and explain that in the West girls wanted to work, and did not expect to be supported by their families until some man came along to take them off their hands.

Her stepfather had not been pleased, but Danielle had persevered, and eventually he had agreed that she might take the Cordon Bleu cookery course she had hoped for.

In her heart she knew that had he realised she hoped to put the expertise she gained to practical use by opening her own restaurant, he would not have been so sanguine. She had a little money of her own left to her by her father, which was invested and would be hers on her twenty-first birthday, in four months' time, and in three weeks she was to start her Cordon Bleu training.

Cookery had been her favourite subject at finishing school; though of course she had enjoyed the lessons in the art of make-up and posture, the shopping trips supervised by the immaculately elegant Frenchwoman who commanded them to choose the clothes they would most like from the expensive boutiques she took them to, and then proceeded to disapprove or approve their choice as the case may be.

Danielle had emerged from finishing school with an instinctive knowledge of what was right for her slender five-foot-four frame, so fine-boned that her fragility caught the breath, and a poise which made her mother sigh and then smile as she realised that her schoolgirl daughter had become a young woman almost overnight.

Most of the other girls at the school had come from wealthy backgrounds, from varied nationalities, but Danielle was unique in being the English stepdaughter of a wealthy Arab.

Like her mother Danille had dark red hair which curled softly on to her shoulders, but whereas her mother's eyes were a pretty, soft blue, Danielle's were green—an inheritance from her Scottish father, her mother had once told her, and they sparkled in her face like green fire, hence her stepfather's statement that he would like to buy her emeralds.

Until her mother's remarriage she and Danielle had lived quite modestly in the small semi in North London which was all she had been able to afford when she had been widowed. It could not have been easy for her mother, Danielle recognised, struggling to bring up a small child on a very slender income, and when Danielle was ten, her mother had been forced to go back to work as a secretary for the oil company where she had eventually met her second husband.

'Are you planning to be in for dinner this evening?' her mother asked, walking into the room.

Although in her early forties, she could easily have passed for Danielle's sister rather than her mother, and Danielle smiled fondly at her. To look at her mother now, wearing an expensively cut couture dress, and discreet jewellery, it was hard to imagine that she had ever wept over the cost of a pair of tights, but Danielle could remember those days, and it was because of them that she was never tempted to take for granted the life-style which was hers now. Although Danielle would never dream of saying so for fear of hurting either of her parents, in many ways she wished her stepfather were not quite so wealthy. She would have loved to share a flat with other girls, struggling to find the rent each month, and enjoying the shared camaraderie of youth, but her parents would have been bitterly hurt had she suggested leaving home, and although he never criticised, Danielle knew that her stepfather, with his Eastern upbringing, rather disapproved of the freedom of some of her friends.

Boys who called to take her out on dates often quailed before his fierce stare, and Danielle had a shrewd suspicion that the combination of his presence and wealth held her escorts' behaviour in check. Certainly, apart from the occasional over-amorous goodnight kiss, she had never had to fight off unwelcome advances. Unless, of course, it was because they didn't find her attractive. The thought made her glance uncertainly into the huge baroque mirror hanging on the wall, a small frown puckering her smooth forehead.

'Well, darling,' her mother persisted, 'will you be joining us for dinner? The Sancerres will be dining with us. They're over from Paris, and Philippe made a special point of asking if you would be in.'

Danielle wrinkled her nose.

Philippe Sancerre was the son of a business colleague of her stepfather's; a Frenchman whom Danielle had met with the rest of his family in Paris the previous year. Philippe was five years older than her, but far more worldly; she had sensed that from the way he had kissed her goodnight after taking her out to dinner. Philippe was very handsome with his smooth brown hair and laughing eyes, but the way he looked at her sometimes made her feel uncomfortable, and she wriggled slightly, remembering it.

She knew all about sex, of course; one could
scarcely not do so nowadays, but knowing and
experiencing were two different things, and so far
her experience was extremely limited—nil almost,
which was a ridiculous state of affairs, she acknowledged wryly. Whoever had heard of a
twenty-one-year-old virgin? It was a secret she
kept very well and intended to go on keeping until
she found the man with whom she could share it.

'Yes, I'll be in for dinner,' she replied, knowing
it was the answer her mother wanted. Another
woman might have resented the presence of such
a young and attractive daughter, but Helen
Hassan loved Danielle too much to feel envy for
her youth. Besides, she had her beloved Hassan.

Danielle applied a touch of sea-green eyeshadow and stood back to study the effect in
her mirror. Her bedroom was furnished with eigh-
teenth-century French antiques, the furniture
gilded and delicate. It had been an eighteenth
birthday present from her stepfather. She had
much to thank him for, she reflected, and not
merely possessions. He had made her mother so
happy. She glowed with that special glow of
women in love, and that he loved her too was very
evident.

The diamond pendant he had given her that
morning flashed fire in the tender valley of her
breasts, lightly confined by the thin silk of her
evening pants suit. The camisole top outlined the
firm thrust of her breasts, before tapering to her
narrow waist.

Her stepfather had never tried to impose
Eastern clothing on either her mother or herself,
but Danielle knew that he preferred her to wear

clothes that were 'modest' and she hoped he would not disapprove of the outfit she was wearing tonight.

That Philippe did not became obvious the moment Danielle stepped into the elegant drawing room. Both he and his father stood up as Danielle entered, but it was Philippe who swiftly crossed the Aubusson carpet to take Danielle's hands in his, imprisoning them while he kissed her warmly.

'Philippe!' Her breathless protest went unheard, Madame Sancerre smiling indulgently as her son stole another kiss before releasing his captive.

'You embarrass Danielle,' she chided him lightly. 'She is not used to such behaviour, is this not so, *petite*?'

Before Danielle could answer Madame Sancerre turned to her mother and said enviously,

'You are fortunate in your daughter, Helen. My Catharine, although three years younger than Danielle, is already a rebel. I have told her more than once that her behaviour is not *comme il faut*; not that which one expects from *une jeune fille bien élevée*, but will she listen? I have told her she will not make a good marriage, but she merely laughs. She does not want to marry, she tells me. She will go to university and qualify as an advocate so that she can support herself.'

Although Madame Sancerre shook her head, Danielle could tell that secretly she was very proud of her daughter. As though he sensed the direction of her thoughts her stepfather came across and put his arm round her shoulders.

'As you say, Madame,' he told the French-woman, 'we are very proud of Danielle. She is everything I have always hoped for in a daughter. Beautiful . . . spirited . . .'

Danielle blushed, and Madame Sancerre laughed. 'A pearl beyond price—you must treasure her greatly, my friend.'

'Very greatly,' her stepfather said, so seriously that Danielle almost protested fearfully that she was human and humanly frail and that he must not put her on such a pedestal, but Madame Sancerre was talking and the moment was lost, forgotten as the conversation became more general.

It was after dinner that Philippe drew Danielle to one side, engaging her in discussion while their elders discussed business in the case of the men and fashion in that of the ladies.

'It is too long since we last met, *chérie*,' he told her. 'You must persuade your stepfather to bring you to Paris with him the next time he comes.'

'I shan't be having much spare time for trips to Paris from now on,' Danielle responded, withdrawing the fingers Philippe was stroking gently. 'I start college soon.'

'College? Oh, you mean your Cordon Bleu course.' You should have taken it in Paris, *chérie*, the home of the only true Cordon Bleu cookery, but I doubt that would suit your papa. He likes to keep his little pearl under his eye, is this not so?'

'He isn't too keen on the idea of me leaving home,' Danielle admitted, 'but one day . . .'

'One day the bird will fly the nest, eh?' Philippe commented with a teasing smile. 'When she does I hope she will fly in my direction. You are very lovely, little Danielle—an enchanting mixture, half women and half child still. When you become all woman, then you will be formidable!'

Danielle had had enough experience of Philippe's flattery to take it with a pinch of salt. He was known to be something of a flirt, and she said so lightly, watching his eyebrows rise in mock pain.

'I a flirt? Never! And certainly not with you, *mignonne*, your stern steppapa would never approve, and my papa is dependent upon him for much of his business. Now, if you are seeking a real Don Juan, a man who is so entirely male that females of the species practically throw themselves at his feet, you can look no farther than the family of your steppapa. Has he told you nothing of Jourdan?' he asked in some surprise when Danielle stiffened slightly 'I can hardly believe it. Jourdan is his favourite nephew.'

'He may have mentioned him—he has so many relatives, I can't remember them all,' Danielle lied, wondering why she should feel this sudden frisson of fear at the mention of the previously unheard-of nephew, Jourdan! It was a strange name, but she wasn't going to betray her curiosity to Philippe's too knowing eyes.

'If he had mentioned him you would surely have remembered it,' Philippe stated positively. 'It is odd that he has not. Hassan and Jourdan are very close. Jourdan is more of a son to him than a nephew.'

Danielle's eyes mirrored her disbelief. If this Jourdan was as close to her stepfather as Philippe claimed how was it that she had never heard of him; never seen him?

An explanation was soon forthcoming.

'Of course, Jourdan did not approve of Hassan marrying your mother,' Philippe told her, 'although I would have thought he would have put all that behind him now. The marriage is fact, and I should have thought Jourdan far too sensible a man to continue to antagonise a man as powerful as Hassan needlessly, especially when he has so much to gain by not antagonising him.'

'Such as what?' Danielle asked. It seemed to her as it had done in the past that her stepfather was not treated as well by his relatives as he ought to be.

Philippe looked at first puzzled and then slightly amused.

'Surely Hassan has told you the story of how he comes to be controlling Qu'Har's oil industry?'

'My stepfather doesn't believe in discussing business with women,' Danielle replied coolly, wishing she did not have to admit this fact. Once she herself would have bridled instinctively at such an insult to the female sex, but she had come to realise that in her stepfather's case his decision sprang more from a misguided desire to protect both Danielle and her mother from worry than a desire to exclude them from that part of his life, although the effect was much the same. Sheikh Hassan was a benevolent autocrat whose care for his womenfolk was unceasing, but Danielle shuddered to think what it must be like to be at the mercy of an Eastern husband who considered women to be on the same plane as domestic pets. Danielle had every European's girl natural desire for independence, but for her stepfather's sake she masked it, unwilling to hurt the man who had done so much for her and her mother.

'That at least is something Jourdan would approve of,' Philippe told her with a smile. 'He is very much what you would term a chauvinist, that one. The last time he came to Paris I was amazed by the low opinion in which he holds your sex, *ma chérie*, and even more amazed by the way your sisters responded to his chauvinism. Of course, power and wealth are a heady combination, and Jourdan has both in full measure, although not in as full a measure as he would wish, perhaps.' He gave Danielle a speculative sideways glance, which she missed as she tried to analyse the intense dislike—almost to the point of hatred—which seemed to be consuming her at the thought of this Jourdan, who apparently despised her sex and made use of it simply for his own pleasure before discarding it like an unwanted suit of clothes.

'You know, of course, that Hassan's father as outright ruler was free to choose which of his sons would rule after him?' Philippe asked Danielle.

She hadn't known, but rather than betray this she nodded and waited for him to go on. In spite of her reservations about letting Philippe confide in her, her curiosity about her stepfather's family could not be denied.

'Sheikh Ben Ibn Ahmed had four sons, of whom Hassan was very obviously his favourite, and would undoubtedly have succeeded him had it not been for the fact that he himself had no sons. With three jealous brothers to contend with Sheikh Ibn Ahmed felt that a man without sons to come after him was not the right choice for ruler of Qu'Har. Nevertheless Hassan was his favourite son, so after consultation with his advisers, the company which controls Qu'Har's oil production and revenues was set up, with Hassan as head of it for his entire lifetime. His choice was a wise one, for under Hassan the company has diversified and grown, and its profits are used to benefit not only his family, but also their people. You may, or may not know that Hassan's ancestors belonged to a small tribe renowned for their ferocity and independence. It was one of my ancestors who persuaded the Sheikh to have his sons educated abroad, by the way, and that is where the connection between Hassan's family and mine comes from. My father says that Hassan has more than repaid whatever his father might have owed my grandfather in the volume of business he puts our way . . .'

'But you don't agree?' Danielle asked shrewdly, noting the discontent suddenly marring his handsome features.

'He has been generous,' Philippe agreed grudgingly, 'but he could be more so. A seat on the board of several of his companies, for instance. It would cost him little, and do much for us.'

As Danielle knew that her stepfather believed that men must earn their way in life by merit, she wisely refrained from answering. Philippe was charming when he had a mind to be, but he did not have the same dedication to work evidenced by his father and hers, and she suspected that as a young man who enjoyed the sophistication of life in Paris, Philippe also wanted the wealth to match his ambitions. She knew that Philippe found her attractive, but she also knew that when he married it would be to a girl of his own class from a wealthy background, a calm and placid Frenchwoman who would turn a blind eye to her husband's other affairs. She could never do that, Danielle acknowledged, a little surprised by the force of her own feelings. When and if she married it would be to a man who loved her as intensely as she loved him, a man who would make her his whole world, just as she would make him hers. She smiled a little sadly. Such men were few and far between. Even her stepfather, who adored her mother, had outside interests which excluded her.

Did her mother know what Philippe had just revealed to her about Hassan's background? she wondered. Surely she must do, and yet she had never spoken to Danielle about it. But then why should she? Danielle admitted. It was only since her return from finishing school that her mother had started to treat her as a woman instead of an adolescent, and she must not forget that to her mother, who had been a mother and a widow at her age, she must seem very young and inexperienced. She didn't feel particularly young, though, Danielle reflected. She had a sensitivity which seemed to draw people with problems to her, and at boarding school and in Switzerland she had often been forced into the position of confidante, lending an ear. Listening to girls confiding to her their problems had given her a greater maturity than most of her peers and she was determined to avoid the pitfalls which seemed to beset them; although, as she freely acknowledged, when the emotions were involved it became hard to stand back and make dispassionate judgments. The one vow she had made to herself which she intended to keep at all costs was to be true to her own code and never to allow anyone to persuade her to compromise it.

'Am I boring you?' Philippe enquired in mock reproof.

Danielle hid a small smile. In point of fact she was very interested in what he was telling her, but she sensed that even had she not been, Philippe's ego would never have allowed him to believe that she was anything other than flattered by his attentions.

'Not at all.' she told him calmly. 'Please go on.'

'There is still the best to come. When Hassan's wife realised that her husband was not to become the ruler of Qu'Har she divorced him—Oh yes, Muslim women have that right under the law of the Koran, although very few of them invoke it. Without a wealthy and powerful family to support them divorced women can have a pretty unpleasant life, but then by all accounts Miriam had never wanted to marry Hassan in the first place. She favoured his elder brother. Hassan refused to take the extra wives the Koran allows him. He knew by then that there would never be any children and told my father that the prospect of running establishments for three quarrelling women appalled him. In addition to giving him absolute control of the oil revenues, Hassan's father also had it written into his will, and witnessed by all his family, that Hassan should be the one to choose his own successor—from among the family, of course; to do otherwise would be unthinkable, but apart from that one proviso Hassan has complete freedom of choice, and until his marriage to your mother it was widely accepted that that choice would be Jourdan, whose own position in the family is somewhat tenuous.'

Although his face was expressionless, from the tone of his voice Danielle gathered that Philippe was somewhat at odds with Jourdan, and wondered why. And then another thought struck her. Was this Jourdan the reason why her step-father had never taken them to Qu'Har or brought any members of his family home? Her resentment against the unknown Jourdan increased. How dared he force a rift between her stepfather and the rest of his family, and for what reason? She knew that many Arabs despised those of their own race who married outside it, but from what Philippe had just told her this Jourdan was in no position to despise his uncle; and certainly not to the extent of promoting a family quarrel.

'Of course none of the family were pleased about the marriage,' Philippe continued. 'After all, Hassan is an extremely wealthy and powerful man, and although it is taken for granted—not without a certain amount of resentment—that Jourdan should inherit Hassan's position and power, the thought of that wealth being shared by yet more foreigners was more than the family could bear.'

Danielle's brain seized on just two words of Philippe's speech, which she repeated disbelievingly. 'More foreigners?'

'Didn't you know?' Philippe asked, plainly enjoying himself. 'Jourdan himself is of mixed blood. In fact he owes his position and acceptance in the family entirely to Hassan. He is the son of Hassan's youngest brother, who was at university

in Paris during his youth. It was there that he
met Jourdan's mother, and Jourdan himself was
conceived, although regrettably without the benefit of marriage. No one in the family knew about
the affair or the child, until Saud was killed in a
street brawl. Hassan went to Paris to sort out his
affairs and discovered that he was living with
Jeannette. When he realised that she was carrying
Saud's child, he offered her money in return for
full legal rights to the baby when it was born.

'Jeannette agreed, and after Jourdan's birth,
Hassan took the baby back to Qu'Har with him.
It was believed within the family that he intended
to bring Jourdan up as the son he himself could
never have, and certainly until he went to school
Jourdan lived in Hassan's household . . .'

Danielle's feeling of injustice that her stepfather
should be treated so ungratefully by a child he
had by all accounts rescued from the gutter overwhelmed her feelings of pity for the small baby so
cavalierly deserted by its mother. How could this
Jourdan, who had obviously been like a son to
her stepfather, now ignore him, and why was
Jourdan never mentioned by her father?

As though he sensed the direction of her
thoughts, Philippe started to supply the answers
to her questions, but before he could say more
than a couple of words her stepfather and
Monsieur Sancerre stood up, and Monsieur
Sancerre called Philippe over to join their discussion.

'These men!' Madame Sancerre said with a
smile when Philippe had gone. 'But there can be
no doubt, *petite*, that Philippe prefers your company to that of his father and the Sheikh.'

When Danielle demurred Madame chided her. 'Oh, come, *chérie*,' she protested, 'you are a very attractive young girl. It cannot have escaped your notice that Philippe finds you attractive?'

CHAPTER TWO

THESE words were repeated, although in a somewhat different vein, the following day when Danielle's stepfather was discussing the events of the previous evening.

'Philippe is pleasant enough,' Danielle agreed sedately, 'but I suspect that he finds all girls who are reasonably pretty, "attractive".' She made a slight moue and her stepfather laughed, ruffling her hair.

'And as a definitely more than "reasonably pretty" girl, you disdain his attentions, is that it?'

He was in a very expansive mood and it struck Danielle that he was relieved that she did not find Philippe attractive. Why? she wondered, and then smiled. Of course, Hassan made no secret of the fact that he liked having her at home and had no doubt feared that she might have taken Philippe's attentions too seriously.

'He is an entertaining companion, nothing more,' she assured him, darting him a glance and wondering if now was the time to mention something which had begun to trouble her lately. She had no wish to hurt her stepfather's feelings, but it was time that he and her mother realised that she was old enough to make her own decisions, run her own life. 'You can't continue to vet all my boy-friends, you know.' she teased, taking a chance that he would take the comment in the spirit in which it was made. 'I'm grown up now!'

The look he gave her was that of a man and not a father, and Danielle flushed defensively as it encompassed her high taut breasts and slender body, before returning to dwell speculatively on her flushed cheeks and sparkling eyes.

'So you are,' he agreed gravely, his voice suddenly serious as he added, 'You know that your happiness is my prime concern, don't you, Danielle?'

When she nodded, he smiled. 'So then there is no need for us to quarrel, is there?'

Weakly agreeing, Danielle was left with the definite sensation that she had been out-manoeuvred.

Her stepfather would have to face up to the fact that she could not live at home for ever, she decided later in the afternoon, preparing for a shopping trip with two friends from finishing school. One of them was training to be a model and the other was a dancer and had just obtained a contract to appear in a West End show. Danielle envied them their free and easy life style, although she was honest enough to admit to herself that the casual procession of men in and out of the lives of some of her friends was not for her. She enjoyed going out with boys and liked them as friends, but somehow she found herself shying away from the thought of a full-blooded affair, even, a little to her own surprise, viewing the idea of such intimacy with a certain amount of distaste. Could she be frigid? She tried to analyse her own instinctive objection to the use of the word, which immediately decried her innate sense of femininity. She would just have to accept that as far as sex was concerned she was a late developer, she decided humorously as she discarded the expensive clothes in her wardrobe in favour of a thin tee-shirt and clinging jeans; either that or she was too romantic, for certainly the thought of sex for sex's sake did nothing for her, and as far as she could ascertain, for her, love must certainly precede the intimacies which other girls had described to her in giggled whispers.

Her friends were an entertaining duo; although coming from relatively wealthy families, they cheerfully searched markets for second-hand clothes of the twenties and thirties, and both, like Danielle herself, were dressed in the ubiquitous jeans and tee-shirts when they met her at the appointed rendezvous. Both girls were full of what they were doing and their plans for the future, and as they described the flat they were sharing and the carefree life they were leading Danielle felt quite envious.

At last Corinne, the dancer, asked her what her plans were for the future, and when told Corinne raised her eyebrows a little.

'A restaurant of your own? That's rather ambitious of you, isn't it? I always had the impression that you were one of those girls who would marry early. In fact I'm surprised you aren't engaged already, especially in view of your background.'

When Danielle looked puzzled she explained lightly, 'Your stepfather, Dan. Don't tell me he doesn't have some eligible man waiting in the wings for you. I mean, in the Middle East the arranged marriage is still very much the thing, isn't it, especially among the wealthy upper classes? A friend of mine was involved with one of them several months ago. She's a girl who's in the show with me, and it's taken her simply ages to get over him. Apparently some of these men are really dynamite, if you're prepared to accept that you'll never be anything to them but something on the side.'

Danielle grimaced, not liking Corinne's expression, descriptive though it was.

'He loaded Vanessa down with jewels and expensive clothes,' Corinne continued, unaware of Danielle's distaste, 'but when it came to the crunch—marriage,' she elucidated when Danielle looked puzzled, 'he told her quite categorically that there was simply no way he was going to marry her. Apparently there was some dutiful little bride already lined up waiting for him. Vanessa was simply furious, and she told him so, but he just laughed at her, apparently. Told her she'd been paid well for the pleasure her body afforded him, but it was over.'

'At least she got something out of it,' Linda observed cynically. 'You hear some pretty unpleasant tales about what can happen to girls who get involved with Muslims in my business. The days are gone when rich Arabs were swept off their feet by fair skin and blonde hair. They've realised that everything has its price, and as everyone ought to know by now, when it comes to bartering they're impossible to beat. Still, if a girl's sensible she can still do quite well—jewellery, holidays, clothes that sort of thing.'

Feeling faintly sickened, Danielle said it was time for her to leave. It was hard to know who offended her innate sense of chastity most—the girl who so cynically sold her body for jewels, or the man who bought it. On balance she thought the man, because he was using the woman for nothing more than momentary satisfaction and thus completely debasing the very foundations of a mutually caring relationship between the two sexes.

'Oh, Vanessa didn't do too badly out of it in that respect,' Corinne agreed carelessly, 'but according to her this Jourdan was quite something, and what she really had in mind was marriage.'

Jourdan! The moment she heard the name Danielle went hot and cold all over. Perhaps it was silly of her to leap immediately to the conclusion that the 'Jourdan' Corinne spoke of was her stepfather's nephew, and yet surely there could not be two wealthy Arabs with that same unusual name.

'Are you okay, Dan?' Corinne asked her with some concern. 'You've gone quite pale.'

'I'm fine,' she lied, collecting her bag and standing up. 'But I ought to be going. I promised my parents I'd be in for dinner tonight.' It was a lie, but all at once it had become imperative to learn more about her stepfather's family, and the only person she could ask was her mother, or failing that, her stepfather himself. On the way home she wondered why she had never thought to question the lack of contact with her stepfather's relatives before; perhaps because she had been away at school so much, so involved in her own life and her own contentment.

She broached the subject over coffee after dinner. Her parents employed a live-in couple, Mr and Mrs Bennett, who acted as chauffeur and cook respectively, and once Mrs Bennett had removed the remains of their meal and they had retired to the drawing room, Danielle merely waited until her mother had poured the rich, sweet coffee her stepfather adored before asking her questions.

'Danielle!' her mother protested when Danielle asked why it was that they had no contact with her stepfather's family.

'No, Helen, she is right to ask,' her husband responded, smiling at Danielle. 'In fact I am surprised that she has not done so before now.'

'I think I was probably too immature, too wrapped up in my own affairs,' Danielle admitted honestly.

'So, and what has prompted this sudden maturity?' Sheikh Hassan queried, his eyes suddenly sharpening. 'Could it have been Philippe Sancerre?'

'Partially,' Danielle admitted, mindful of her stepfather's business relationship with Philippe's family and not wishing to prejudice it by making him angry with Philippe. 'But I think that living at home as I'm doing now has made me realise how isolated we are.'

'Well, I can tell you the main reason,' Danielle's mother began. 'Ahmed's family did not approve of his marriage to me. Oh, they were quite within their rights,' she added before Danielle could object. 'After all, what did they know of me? Your stepfather has had to give up a great deal to be with us, Danny.'

The reversion to her baby name made Danielle smile a little, her own eyes misting over as she saw the tears in her mother's as she turned to her husband.

'My family were wilfully and blindly pre-judiced,' he said softly. 'And never for a moment doubt that I have not treasured every second of my life with you, Helen.' His free arm came out to encircle Danielle. 'The happiness the two of you have brought to my life has enriched it like rain to the parched desert.'

'And now we shall be even happier,' Danielle's mother said with a smile. She turned to Danielle. 'Hassan's family want a reconciliation.'

'Even Jourdan?' Danielle could not resist saying a little bitterly.

Her stepfather's protective arm dropped and it seemed to her that her parents exchanged a look which excluded her totally; a look which made her blood run cold with a nameless fear.

'What do you know of Jourdan?' her stepfather asked her quietly.

'Only that he didn't want you to marry my mother; that he considers women to be animated toys designed specifically for his pleasure, and that when he's finished with them he throws them aside like so many unwanted empty cartons.'

'Jourdan is of the desert,' her stepfather said, without making any attempt to deny her words. 'He has its strength and endurance, and perhaps a little of its cruelty, but there is another side to him. No man can live as the hawk for all his life; there comes a time always when he needs the softness of the dove; when even the fiercest heart cries out for the tranquillity of the oasis. In Jourdan, it is true that this side is well hidden. I will not ask where you learned so much of my nephew,' Sheikh Hassan added, 'for I believe I already know the answer. It is not always wise to

allow the hawk and the sparrow to grow up together, for the sparrow will always seek to taint
the nobility of his fellow, knowing its lack in himself.'

'Philippe is not a sparrow,' Danielle protested,
shocked by the cynical twist of her stepfather's
lips.

'No? Were you aware that his father had approached me for your hand in marriage on
Philippe's behalf?'

Even as she absorbed the formally old-
fashioned words Danielle's shocked face betrayed
that she had not.

'Danielle.' Her stepfather's arm round her
shoulders comforted her distress. 'You must not
blame him too much. Philippe is a young man
with expensive tastes, and as the daughter of an
extremely wealthy man—and a very, very beautiful daughter, of course, Philippe has the sybarite's
love of beauty as well as wealth—a man who
already has business connections with his father,
what could be more natural than that his practical
French mind should turn towards marriage?'

'I thought he liked *me*,' Danielle murmured
bleakly. 'I had no idea . . .'

'But you did not love him? There had been no
intimacy between you?'

Danielle heard her mother's small protest above
the sharpness in her stepfather's voice and
regained enough of her normal calm independence to say sardonically,

'Fortunately, no.' She turned to her mother
with a bleak smile. 'How lucky you've been, darling. Two men have loved you—if all the men I
meet are going to turn out like Philippe and

Jourdan, I doubt if I'll ever find one to love me.'

'Jourdan? Why do you mention him?' her step-father demanded, while Danielle was still trying to come to terms with her own admission to her-self. She did want someone to love her, and to love him in return. She was obviously not as in-dependent as she thought, and not for the first time she wished that her parents' care of her had not been quite so protective. She might feel just the same as other girls her age, but in many ways she was not, and she was forced to admit that her view of love had probably been too coloured by her stepfather's obvious adoration of her mother. She knew that he was probably unique among his own race, but she was now beginning to wonder if he was not also unique among men in general.

She gathered her thoughts hurriedly, aware that her stepfather was still awaiting her reply. Something about the look in his eyes made her lift her head proudly and say, 'Isn't it true that he's betrothed to some poor girl who has to accept him in marriage whether she wants to or not; some girl who's most probably kept in ignorance of her fate, and the manner in which her prospective husband conducts himself?'

'You would condemn a man purely on the con-viction of one other, who is known to be envious of him?' her stepfather asked mildly. 'I had thought better of you, Danielle.'

'It wasn't just Philippe,' she retorted, resenting her stepfather's knack of making her feel guilty, especially when she had nothing to feel guilty for.

'Some friends of mine happened to mention him—quite by chance, they had no idea that I knew him. They were telling me about a girl he'd been involved with in Paris.'

Her stepfather made an abrupt disdainful gesture. 'A *putain*; a woman of the world who gives her body in return for gain . . .'

'It doesn't matter what she was,' Danielle protested hotly, 'she was still a person, a human being with feelings. If men were not prepared to buy then women wouldn't sell . . .'

It was plain that her stepfather did not agree with her.

'A man has needs,' he said frankly, 'and when he can slake them nowhere else he will queue in the market-place and buy water. Of course, it will not have the fresh sweetness of water from his own private oasis; it will taste brackish and perhaps not refresh, but it is still water. I had thought you more generous, Danielle, than to condemn a man purely because he indulges a perfectly natural appetite . . .'

Danielle turned away, suddenly close to tears. For all their love for one another she and her stepfather were miles apart. She sensed that were she to say to him, 'What of women's needs; is their "thirst" to be slaked in the same fashion?' he would have been honestly shocked and distressed. It was the old double standard, she told herself bitterly, but her sex wasn't merely enchained by what men expected of it, it was also enchained by its own emotions, for whereas a man could take merely out of need, a woman could rarely give without emotion, without giving something of herself. It isn't fair, she wanted to protest rebelliously, but instead she summoned all her powers of reasoning and logic and said calmly,

'Naturally any man could be forgiven one lapse, but from what I hear your nephew, far from restraining his "thirst" having slaked it once, encourages it to grow stronger. As I said before, I sincerely pity the poor girl who is destined to be his wife. Or one of his wives, I should say.'

'Then you would be wrong.' Her stepfather said coolly. Danielle thought she discerned a mixture of pain and admiration in his eyes, but overriding both emotions was a determination which sent prickles of primitive awareness running along her body until the tiny hairs at the nape of her neck and along her arms rose as defensively as the prickles of a hedgehog.

'Jourdan can only take one wife. I assume you already know the story of his birth from Philippe, but what you obviously do not know is the promise I had to give his mother before I was allowed to take him from her—namely that he was to be brought up in the Christian religion. Even though she died several days after his birth, I adhered to that promise, and despite his prominence in Qu'Har my nephew is as Christian as you yourself, Danielle.'

Then all the more shame to him, Danielle wanted to cry, but for some reason her tongue seemed to have cleaved to the roof of her mouth. A curious sense of unreality enveloped her, a feeling of foreboding, intensified by the anxious look in her mother's eyes whenever they rested upon her.

'As my adopted daughter, you will one day be extremely wealthy,' Sheikh Hassan continued, completely changing the subject. 'We have never talked of this before because the subject has not arisen. As you know, I am an extremely rich man, but I also own and control much family property which can only be passed down from father to son, from brother to brother, or uncle to nephew. There is no female right of inheritance. Were I to die my own private fortune would be divided between your mother and yourself, but my controlling interest in the oil company would go to either my older or my younger brother, since I have no sons of my own. The balance of power in Qu'Har is poised delicately between my brothers, both are intensely jealous of each other, and it sometimes takes the wisdom of Solomon to make them see reason, but were I to die and my share of the oil company not be willed away from them, civil war would surely break out in our small country, and thus would follow the destruction of everything my father, and myself after him, have striven for.

'In addition to this I must make provision for your own safety. On my death you will be very, very wealthy; you have had a sheltered upbringing, and know little of men; it is my great fear that you might fall into the hands of one who will mistreat or abuse you, Danielle, purely through greed.'

He made her sound like an over-ripe fruit, Danielle thought half hysterically. Could he really believe she was so incapable of managing her own affairs?

'If you believe that, it might be kinder not to leave me anything at all,' she pointed out logically with a smile. 'In some ways I would rather you didn't. I should like to succeed on my own merits . . .'

Her stepfather's expression softened at the

youthful words and earnest expression on the mobile face before him. She was too beautiful for her own good, this adopted daughter of his, with skin like milk and eyes as green as precious stones.

'You are a wise child, Danielle, who already sees the burdens of great wealth and will never abuse its privileges, but you have no need to worry, I have already made provision both for the protection of my controlling share of the oil company and you and the fortune you will one day own . . .' He looked at his wife, and a look seemed to pass between them; seeking on his part, and accepting on hers, but totally excluding Danielle. Tension tightened her stomach muscles and a dread she could not understand washed over her like icy cold water.

'How?'

The word was a husky plea, mirrored, although she did not know it, by the expression in her eyes.

Her stepfather came to her and took both her hands in his, his eyes kind.

'There is nothing to fear, little dove. Jourdan knows what a pearl beyond price he is getting in the greatest treasure I own, and he will treat you accordingly . . . When you are his wife all this . . .'

Danielle reeled, hearing nothing more than those fateful words, 'When you are his wife . . .' *She* was the poor unsuspecting girl who was expected to marry Jourdan, and now she knew why.

'Danielle?'

It was her mother's voice, soft and anxious. She

forced herself to fight off the faintness threatening to overwhelm her and respond to it.

'I'm fine,' her voice gathered strength, 'But I will not marry Jourdan. I'd rather starve!'

The moment the words left her mouth Danielle realised how childish they sounded; how pre-judicial they were to her intended claim that she was old enough by far to decide the course of her own life.

'Mummy, surely you can understand?' she pleaded.

'Of course, darling,' her mother soothed, glanc-ing anxiously towards her husband. 'But Hassan merely wants to do what is best for you.' She touched her daughter gently on the arm and smiled faintly. 'You know, Danny, you've had such a sheltered life that your father and I only wanted to protect you . . .'

'Oh, Mother!' Danielle sighed, unconsciously deliberately not using the more childish 'Mummy', 'you can't keep me wrapped in cotton wool for ever, you know—and besides; from what I've already heard of him marriage to Jourdan would be far from a bed of roses.'

'You must take what Philippe Sancerre told you with a pinch of salt,' her stepfather said calmly. 'While I cannot attempt to speak for Jourdan's past, Danielle, like all men of good sense he knows that marriage is a serious business, and once married . . .'

'It doesn't matter how seriously he takes it,' Danielle interrupted swiftly, 'and it wouldn't alter my views in the slightest if we were talking of some other man; personalities do not enter into my argument, I object to the principle of the arranged marriage, no matter how or why it arises. Oh, I know you have only my welfare at heart, but such a marriage is abhorrent and repugnant to me. I could no more agree to it than I could . . . fly!'

'I understand how you feel, darling,' her mother said gently. 'Hassan, try to understand,' she appealed to her husband. 'Although Danielle has had a sheltered upbringing, she is not a Muslim girl trained from birth to accept male dominance and her role in life unquestioningly.'

'And nor should I wish her to be,' Danielle's stepfather agreed, smiling fondly at the downbent darkened head and rebelliously taut body of his stepdaughter.

'Then you accept that there can be no marriage between your nephew and myself?' Danielle asked him.

'If that is your wish, but I cannot pretend that I am not disappointed. It would have been a good marriage. Jourdan will have to be told, of course . . .'

'I'm sure he'll soon find someone else,' Danielle said grimly, remembering the girl Corinne had mentioned.

'When it becomes known in our family that he is not to marry you, he will lose face,' her stepfather said sombrely, 'but the fault is perhaps mine. I forgot that for all I consider you to be my daughter, you are not, as your mother does well to remind me, a daughter of the East . . .'

He looked so cast down that Danielle was moved to comfort him. 'I know you were trying to secure my future, but when I marry I want it to be to a man I can respect and share my life with, not a man who looks to me only to bear his children. Besides,' she added firmly, 'I'm not ready for marriage . . .'

For the second time in a very short span of hours her stepfather's wryly encompassing scrutiny of her slender, determined form filled her with embarrassment.

'Perhaps not yet,' he agreed. 'But the time is not far off . . . If you will not marry Jourdan, then will you at least visit my family as my emissary? As you know, I shall shortly have to go to America on business. Your mother will come with me, and it would please me greatly, Danielle, if you would use these weeks before you start college—if that is what you are determined to do—to show my family how beautiful and chaste a daughter I have.'

'You mean fly out to Qu'har?' Danielle asked. 'Oh, but I couldn't . . .' Couldn't live with complete strangers, was what she meant, strangers who disapproved of her mother and her marriage to their relative; strangers who included the man she had just refused to marry!

It was later when she was preparing for bed that her mother entered her room, so quietly that at first Danielle didn't hear her.

'Danielle,' her mother begged softly, sitting down on Danielle's bed, and watching her daughter brush the gleaming cloud of darkened curls clustering on her shoulders, 'please go to Qu'Har. It means so much to Hassan—far more than he has told you. You have compassion and imagination, surely you can understand how bitter has been his own lack of children, especially in view of his position? To claim you as his daughter, albeit by marriage, is one of his greatest joys. Do not deny him the pleasure of showing you off to his family . . .'

'A family who don't want anything to do with us as long as Daddy continues to make money for them,' Danielle protested rebelliously, putting down her brush and turning to face her mother. 'I can't do it. I can't pretend the way I would have to . . .'

'Not even for the sake of your father?' her mother prodded gently. 'It would be a compromise, Danny. I know Hassan mentioned that Jourdan will lose face over your refusal to marry him, but so will Hassan . . .'

Her sympathy aroused in spite of her own feelings, Danielle stared reluctantly at the floor, knowing what her mother was asking of her and yet unwilling to commit herself to visiting Qu'Har.

'I can understand Daddy,' she said at last. 'But you . . . surely you knew that I would never agree to such a marriage?'

'I knew, but Hassan was so sure he was doing the right thing, so convinced that he was protecting you that only your own reaction could convince him. Having gained so much surely you can afford a little compromise now, darling?'

CHAPTER THREE

A LITTLE compromise took one a long, long way,
Danielle thought ruefully, staring out of the
window of the powerful jet—one of the twelve
owned by Qu'Har Air. This jet, though, was
special. It was the personal property of her stepfather's family, and a courteous, deferential young
man had been conscripted from his normal job in
the oil company offices to accompany her to
Qu'Har.

The whine of the high-powered engines
changed abruptly, denoting the fact that they were
nearing their destination. In spite of her resolu-
tion not to be, Danielle felt nervous. She
smoothed the skirt of the silk two-piece she was
wearing with fingers that trembled slightly. The
silk was peacock green, highlighting her hair and
flattering the golden tones the summer sun had
given her skin. She eyed it ruefully. Never in all
her holidays abroad had she ever tanned. When
she had complained about it to a beautician the
girl had chided her, telling her she ought to be
grateful for having such a delicate English complexion and preserve it at all costs. The colour in
it now was only as a result of slow and careful
exposure over the entire length of a particularly
good English summer, and her stepfather had told
her that even though the worst of the humidity
had passed the temperature in Qu'Har in August
was very high, and would continue to be high

throughout the duration of her stay. For this reason she had been careful to include in her packing a good supply of sunscreen, essential if her skin wasn't to get badly burned. The girl in the chemist's had also suggested a new sunburn lotion which she had assured Danielle was extremely effective, and that too had been packed with her other cosmetics just in case.

What would her stepfather's family think of her? Although she assured herself that she couldn't care less, for his sake she knew that she hoped they would approve of her. Jourdan, thank goodness, would be in Paris, on business, or so she had been told, and she was grateful to her stepfather who she was sure had been responsible for this diplomatic move. It would have been awkward and embarrassing to have to meet the man who had so callously agreed to marry her, without even seeing her, and she was glad that she would not be called upon to do so.

The jet was descending; she glanced out of the window but could see nothing apart from dazzling blue sky. As she glanced back Danielle saw that her escort was watching her shyly, although he looked hurriedly away when he realised that she had observed his speculative glance. He was about her own age dressed expensively in a Western style suit, his black hair neatly groomed. He was, her stepfather had told her, the son of one of his cousins, in addition to being on the staff of the oil company. In Arab countries nepotism was obviously a virtue rather than a vice, and as the jet came to rest on the tarmac runway Danielle wished that she had had time to study the life style and customs of the people with whom she would be living, a little more thoroughly. What if she transgressed against some unknown rule and disgraced herself? Hassan's eldest brother's first wife would take her under his wing, her stepfather had told her, adding that she would like Jamaile, who had already brought up three daughters and had several grandchildren.

More grateful than she was prepared to admit for the presence of the shy young man at her side, Danielle descended the gangway. The staff were lined up at the bottom. The captain asked if she had enjoyed the flight. Although she had been accustomed to the respect people accorded wealth, she had never known the true meaning of the word 'deference' until she became a member of the Ahmed family, Danielle acknowledged; realising with a sudden startled shock that she *was* a member of that family, even if only by marriage.

That thought gave her the courage to walk calmly to the waiting limousine—no other words could describe the sleek black Mercedes parked prominently on the forecourt flying pennants which Danielle decided must reflect the status of her host and hostess. It was only just beginning to dawn on her that she would be staying with Qu'Har's Royal Family, and the realisation intimidated her a little.

The drive to the palace was completed in silence—an awed one on Danielle's part as she observed the number and variety of buildings being erected on either side of the main road. Beyond them stretched the vast emptiness of the desert broken only by the odd clump of palm trees, until suddenly, quite out of the blue, they came to a vast acreage of tunnel greenhouses, which she was told were part of a new scheme to decrease Qu'Har's dependence on imports from abroad.

'This and the new desalination plant just completed on the coast are the result of Sheikh Hassan's wishes that our people share in the oil wealth of our country,' Danielle's escort told her proudly. And it was something to be proud of, Danielle acknowledged, observing the signs of technology all around her.

One particularly light airy building was pointed out to her as a new girls' school—a very daring innovation and one which had caused considerable tension and high feeling until the country's religious leaders had given the ambitious scheme their approval. Even so, Danielle caught the hint of disapproval in the voice of her young escort.

'You don't approve of education for women?' she asked him directly.

Colour ran up under his dark skin. Danielle would have had to be blind to be unaware of the admiration in his dark eyes as they rested on her, but apart from being mildly flattered that such a handsome young man should so obviously find her attractive she didn't give the matter another thought.

'It is not the way of the East,' was the only diplomatic response she could get to her question, and sensing that he would prefer not to pursue a subject which obviously embarrassed him, Danielle turned instead to his family and in particular those members of it with whom she would be staying.

'The Emir is the head of our family and our

country,' Saud confided with a shy smile. 'I am the son of his second cousin and thus of minor importance within the family. Indeed it was only through the good offices of Sheikh Hassan, my uncle, that I obtained my position with the oil company.'

'But you have a university degree,' Danielle persisted, remembering what her stepfather had told her about this personable young man. 'You could have obtained a job elsewhere . . .'

'I should not have wanted to. Qu'Har is my home and the home of my fathers before me. Sheikh Hassan paid for my education, as he has done for many of us, and it is only fitting that I repay him by using my skills for the benefit of my country.'

It was said so simply, so without pretension and priggishness, that Danielle felt tears prick her eyes. This was the other side of the fierce desert warrior, this almost childlike simplicity and determined loyalty.

'Sheikh Hassan is a generous and wise man,' Saud added seriously. 'Many within our family have reason to be grateful to him.'

'Especially Jourdan,' Danielle added, thinking of how her stepfather had rescued and brought up the small child.

'Ah, Jourdan,' Saud said warmly, so warmly that Danielle glanced at him, surprised to see a look almost approaching worship in the liquid eyes. 'My father says that he is the natural successor to Sheikh Hassan and that without him our country would be torn to shreds and thrown to the winds. He is what in our family we call "The gift of the Prophet".'

Danielle thought he was referring to a discreet way of describing Jourdan's illegitimacy until he saw the look of solemn reverence on his face.

' "The Gift of the Prophet?" What is that?' she asked, curious, in spite of her aversion for the man who would have married her without thought or compunction.

'Quite simply the birth of one with the power, the knowledge and the skill to hold our people together,' Saud told her seriously. 'Always such a one is born to our ruling house in times of conflict and need. Sheikh Hassan himself was thought to be such a gift by his father until it was realised that he could not father children. You must know that in a family such as ours with many brothers and sons there is always fierce rivalry. Sometimes that rivalry breaks out in warfare as rival factions battle for control.

'We are only a small country, but very rich in oil. Unfortunately our people sometimes lack the education to use wealth wisely. It is important that we plan now for the future when we may no longer have our oil, and that is what Sheikh Hassan is trying to do. Many schemes have been launched, many of our brighter young men educated abroad, and much money spent in technological equipment and learning, but all this will be wasted if there is no one to continue Sheikh Hassan's work when he is gone. It must be a man strong enough to quell opposition, fierce as the hawk and wily as the snake. Jourdan is such a man . . .'

He sounded very unpleasant, Danielle thought distastefully. 'Fierce as the hawk.' That no doubt meant domineering and aggressive. 'Wily as the snake.' She conjured up a picture of a Machiavellian mind capable of all manner of intrigue. She already knew how much the Muslim mind appreciated subtlety and how necessary it was to have this gift in full measure if one were to succeed in the Arab business world. The Arab would not respect a man he could cheat, and respect was all-important.

'You obviously admire him,' Danielle said in a neutral voice, wondering if Saud was aware of the marriage her stepfather had planned for her. In view of Jourdan's importance it was strange that a full-blooded Arab girl from within the Royal Family had not been chosen for him, and she realised for the first time that her stepfather had been trying to confer a great favour (in the eyes of his family at least) upon her by this marriage.

'I do,' Saud agreed. 'Although it is thought by some that his adherence to the religion of his mother is foolish. However, the Koran acknowledges the worth of other religions, and Jourdan accepts the precepts of the Koran and abides by them far more stricly than many of our race.'

'He sounds quite a paragon,' Danielle said dryly, her dislike of the unknown Jourdan growing by the minute. 'What a shame that I shall not meet him . . .'

She was too busy studying the scenery beyond the window to see the swift, startled sideways glance Saud gave her. They were driving up to an archway set in a high white wall, the white paint glittering so brightly in the brilliant sunshine that Danielle had to close her eyes against the glare.

When she opened them again the huge car had come to rest in front of a long, low building, its windows all shuttered like so many closed eyes, the delicate mosaic work adorning the gateway making her gasp with pleasure.

'I must leave you here,' Saud announced, climbing out of the car. 'The driver will take you round to the women's quarters where you will be received by the Sheikha.'

'Will I see you again?'

All at once he had become an important link with home and all things familiar. Saud flushed and seemed to glance hesitantly at the driver as though reluctant for him to overhear their conversation.

'It may be permitted. I shall ask my father,' he muttered in a low voice, and then the car was sweeping away through another archway decorated with a continuous frieze of arabesques and into a courtyard enclosed on all four sides.

A door in one wall opened inwards, and feeling rather Alice in Wonderlandish, Danielle realised that she was supposed to get out of the car and enter the building.

She did so like someone in a dream, aware of activity behind her as another door in the adjacent wall opened and the car boot was opened and her luggage removed.

As she stepped through the open door, the scent of jasmine immediately enveloped her, together with a welcome coolness which she realised was stimulated by the powerful air-conditioning whose hum she could just faintly hear.

'If the Sitt will follow me.'

The girl was draped from head to foot in black, her voice low and melodious, and Danielle could just catch the faint chime of ankle bracelets

as she swayed down the corridor in front of her.
At the bottom she opened a door and indicated
that Danielle was to follow. She found herself in
a small square room with a low divan under one
window and a small sunken pool just beyond it.

'If the Sitt will permit.'

Gently but inexorably Danielle was pushed
down on to the divan, her high-heeled sandals
removed. She was glad that she was not wearing
tights when the girl promptly proceeded to wash
her hands and feet with water from the pool, again
scented with some elusive perfume which drifted
past her nostrils and refused to be properly
identified.

The girl's movement were deft and sure, her
hands delicately hennaed and her eyes modestly
downcast all the time. She must be a maid,
Danielle reflected when she walked across to the
other side of the room and returned with a pair of
soft embroidered slippers.

'It is necessary to wear these in the presence of
the Sheikha,' the girl explained. 'It is the custom
to kneel and approach, and then to leave the room
backwards, but in your case it is necessary only to
kneel. For you the Sheikha has waived the normal
formalities . . .'

The girl's English was perfect, so perfect that
Danielle felt ashamed of her own lack of Arabic.
She had learned it from her father, she explained
when Danielle questioned her, and had been fortunate enough to get her position in the Sheikha's
household because of it, because the Sheikha
wanted all her daughters and granddaughters to
speak it.

'It is necessary when they go to school in

England,' she added. 'The Sheikha wishes the
women of her family to have the benefit of a good
education. She says it is important that the women
of our race do not cause our menfolk to have a
contempt of them because of their ignorance. I
shall take you to her now, if you will please follow
me.'

The room they were in was an ante-room leading into a huge chamber with a vaulted, carved
and painted ceiling, the intricacy of the arabesques and stylised carvings on the ceiling taking
away Danielle's breath; and the colours! Never
had she seen such a multitude of rich, jewel-bright
colours all in one room before, and yet as her eyes
became accustomed to the richness she realised
that they were carefully and subtly arranged so
that turquoise ran into lilac and rich purple into
crimson, into royal blue and back to turquoise,
the skilful blending shown to its best advantage
on the plain off-white divans placed around the
room and covered with multi-coloured silk cushions.

At one end of the room was a raised dais with a
single divan on it, and behind the divan was a
delicately   carved   and   scrolled   screen   that
reminded Danielle of photographs she had seen
of Russian iconostases, although of course these
were not of a religious nature, nor did they depict
the human form, relying entirely on colour for
their beauty. Semi-precious stones studded into
the screen glittered in the sunlight pouring in
through the narrow slits left by the closed shutters, and as Danielle collected herself she realised
that her companion had quietly left the room and
that she was all alone.

A door in the screen started to open and re-membering the maid's whispered instructions Danielle knelt hastily on the small mat placed strategically in front of her on the beautifully tiled floor.

She heard a soft chiming sound, and the rustle of heavy silk but dared not lift her head, and then a pleasant voice commanded softly,

'Come here, child, and let us see this daughter of whom my brother Hassan is so proud.'

Danielle stood up and walked hesitantly to-wards the dais. The woman seated on it was tiny, the rich silk of her caftan burnished by the thin light, the jewels on her fingers and round her plump throat making Danielle gasp in awe.

'She has hair the colour of the desert after rain,' the Sheikha commented to one of the women clustered behind her. Danielle had been oblivious to their presence until the Sheikha spoke, having eyes only for the diminutive woman on the divan.

'Such hair colour is an indication of a swift temper in England,' one of the women replied softly, but not so softly that Danielle couldn't hear her.

The Sheikha smiled, and indicated that Danielle was to mount the dais.

'How fortunate then are English men,' she said dryly, 'for unlike our men who must judge by repute alone, one look indicates whether they have a wife of spirit, as temperamental as an Arab mare, or one with the docility of a courtyard dove. Which do you think a man would prefer?' she demanded, looking at Danielle with shrewd brown eyes.

Thrown off guard, all Danielle could say was, 'I don't know. I suppose men like women have different needs. Some prefer placid women and some spirited.'

'She speaks wisely,' the Sheikha said to her women, 'And Hassan has not lied, her beauty is that of the waterlily which flowers in our pools, pale and delicate, curling in on itself when threatened. While you remain in Qu'Har you will live amongst my household,' the Sheikha told Danielle. 'As Hassan has no doubt told you, it is not permitted for our women to walk unescorted in the streets, nor to go unveiled in the presence of men other than their fathers and husbands. Naturally as a European you would not be expected to observe these rules, but as the daughter of our brother you would reflect upon his standing were you to be seen flouting them. The choice is yours, Danielle. Should you wish to adopt our customs while you live among us Zoe will provide you with a *chadrah* and instruct you in the laws of our country, but should you prefer to retain the customs of the West this we shall quite understand.'

Choice? What choice? Danielle wondered with a certain amount of grim bitterness as she acknowledged the shy smile of the girl the Sheikha had indicated. Were she to insist on wearing her own clothes she would be branded as selfish and uncaring of her stepfather's reputation, but were she to dress and behave as an Arab girl it would be tantamount to denying her own personality.

Everyone was waiting for her to speak. She remembered all the generosity and love her stepfather had given her, and acknowledged that there was only one thing she could say.

'I shall wear the *chadrah*', she said bleakly, suddenly overwhelmed by a feeling of presience so strong that she immediately wanted to recall the words. It was as though she had committed herself to an alien uncharted course; as though her life would never be the same again simply by the speaking of that one sentence. Don't be so silly, she chided herself. All she was doing was ensuring that none of Hassan's family would ever again have cause to criticise his choice of second wife!

The Sheikha smiled.

'So be it. Go with Zoe. We shall talk again, you and I. It is many years since I have seen Hassan and you will tell me all about England which I have not visited since I was a girl.'

Remembering that she was supposed to back out of the room, Danielle moved slowly away from the dais, earning an approving smile from Zoe who was at her side.

Once outside the audience chamber, as Zoe told her the room was called, she led Danielle back down a long corridor.

'A suite of rooms has been prepared for you. . . .'

They went up a flight of spiral stairs which seemed to go on for ever, Zoe pausing on the landing for Danielle to catch up with her before opening a door.

A suite, she had called it! Danielle stared round at her palatial surroundings in mingled bemusement and awe, following Zoe like a sleepwalker as she led her from the exquisite salon to a sumptuous bedroom, the low bed draped in silk coverings which closed over it very much in the fashion of a fourposter, but far more delicate and gilded with what Danielle recognised to her astonishment was gold leaf. Beyond the bedroom was a small dressing room lined with mirror-fronted wardrobes, an obviously modern innovation, and beyond that a bathroom with sunken bath, shower and other sanitary fitments, all in a delicate pale pink marble to match the colour scheme in the bedroom.

'The maid will bring you some caftans to choose from,' Zoe announced when the tour was finished. 'And then tomorrow the dressmaker will call and you will be able to choose exactly what you want . . .'

'I shall only be here for three weeks,' Danielle protested weakly. 'It really isn't necessary, Zoe.'

'To refuse the Sheikha's gift is to insult her,' Zoe said seriously.

'Oh, well, in that case . . .'

Zoe spent half an hour with her going through a few basic do's and don'ts, her smile kind when Danielle stopped her, protesting that she would never remember everything she had been told.

'It is not as hard as you imagine,' Zoe comforted her. 'And one of us will be with you always to help you . . . I shall see you again at the evening meal,' she added, rising lithely from the divan. 'You remember the way?'

Assuring her that that at least was something she would not forget, Danielle watched the door closing behind her, feeling rather forlorn. Despite the disparity in their cultures and upbringing she liked Zoe, with her gentle eyes and soft voice. She was the Sheikha's niece, she had explained to Danielle, and had been chosen to be one of the

Sheikha's attendants, much to her family's delight, for it was a very great honour, and if the Sheikha was pleased with her at the end of her year's service she would reward her by adding handsomely to her dowry and helping her parents to find her a good husband.

Danielle had been aghast by these revelations, but Zoe seemed to find nothing to question in them, happily accepting her father's right to find and choose her marriage partner. Nothing had been said about her proposed marriage to Jourdan, and Danielle wisely kept silent, surmising that it was not generally known.

When Zoe had gone Danielle examined the contents of the wardrobe Zoe had discreetly pointed out to her. Half a dozen jewelled silk caftans wafted gently in the draught from the opening doors, their colours ranging from palest pink to deepest jade green. She lifted one out and held it against her, surprised to discover how the Oriental robe transformed her from a neat European into a sultry Easterner. It must surely have been a trick of the light which gave her lips that sultry pout, she decided, hastily replacing the caftan with the others. There was a gentle knock on the door and when Danielle went to answer it a young girl stood there, eyes modestly downcast.

'The Sheikha has sent me to attend the Sitt,' the girl said, stepping into the room. 'She has also sent you this *chadrah* so that you will be able to conceal yourself as you walk about the palace.'

Danielle took the thick, black, enveloping cloak with thinly concealed distaste, shrinking away from the thought of wearing a garment whose sole purpose was in such direct opposition to her own

principles, but she was here in many ways as her
stepfather's emissary, she reminded herself, and
rather than cause offence she would wear the tent-
like garment. She was only grateful that the fast-
ing month of Ramadan was past, she was just
thinking, when the high, thin sound of the
muezzin broke the silence, startling her to such an
extent that she dropped the cloak.

The maid prostrated herself immediately, remaining prone for several seconds before rising
calmly with lithe grace and walking over to
Danielle.

'You will want to bathe before the evening
meal, and I shall attend you. The Sheikha has
sent some perfumed oil for you made from the
roses of her own garden. You are greatly
honoured.'

Danielle wanted to protest uncomfortably that
she did not need any help, but the girl was already
walking through into the sumptuous bathroom,
running the water and pouring something from a
small vial into the marble depths, which immediately turned the water milky.

'I can manage by myself,' Danielle began, but
the girl's expression was so puzzled and hurt that
Danielle found herself relenting when she asked
if Danielle meant to send her away.

'European girls are not used to having a personal maid,' Danielle tried to explain, asking the
girl her name.

'Zanaide,' she replied shyly. 'The Sheikha will
think I have offended you in some way if the Sitt
sends me away . . .'

The huge brown eyes looked so mournful that
Danielle hadn't the heart to insist, but her British

heritage told her there was something vaguely sybaritic about lying full length in the deliciously scented water while Zanaide's small hennaed hands gently sponged her body, but by the time she was ready to step out of the bath and into the towel Zanaide was holding for her, Danielle was beginning to feel her inhibitions completely slipping away, until Zanaide commented admiringly on the colour and texture of her skin.

'So white and soft! The man who looks upon such beauty must surely be blinded by it—but the Sitt must eat more and gain flesh.'

'In European countries men prefer their women to have less flesh,' Danielle explained with a wry smile, guessing the direction Zanaide's thoughts had taken.

'The Sitt is not already betrothed?'

Somehow the personal nature of the questions had ceased to bother Danielle. She shook her head, still smiling.

'Are you betrothed, Zanaide?'

The little maid nodded firmly.

'For many years, to my second cousin, as is the custom. We are to be married next year.' She sighed, standing up, whisking away the protection of the towel before Danielle could protest and opening a small cupboard. 'If the Sitt will lie on the divan, please . . .'

Bemused, Danielle did as she was bid, protesting halfheartedly as she caught the elusive perfume of the oil Zanaide was deftly massaging into her body.

'I have not seen Faisal for many years,' Zanaide told her. 'He has been at university in England and then working in Saudi Arabia, but my brother tells me he has grown into a handsome young man.' A tiny dimple appeared by her mouth and Danielle smiled in response. So not all the spirit had been crushed out of these women whom legend described as frail and delicate as rose petals but who in reality needed the courage and stamina of a lioness.

'And you do not mind this arranged marriage?' Danielle asked her curiously. 'You do not wish that you might have fallen in love, chosen your own husband?'

'I shall fall in love with my husband,' Zanaide responded firmly. 'To do otherwise would be to disgrace my family.'

She left the room for a few minutes, returning with the jade green caftan on one arm.

'Not that one!' Danielle wanted to protest, remembering how shocked she had been by that brief image of herself in it earlier, but Zanaide frowned, and insisted,

'This one is the best in the cupboard. To refuse to wear it would be to insult the Sheikha. You do not like it?'

'It's gorgeous,' Danielle admitted. 'But I feel more at home in my own clothes, just as you would feel uncomfortable in mine.'

To her surprise Zanaide laughed, her eyes twinkling.

'I wear the jeans too, Sitt, but only at home with my mother and sisters. My mother is shocked, but my brothers tell her that in Europe all girls wear them. It is very pleasant to do this, to—what is it you say? Have the best of two worlds.'

'Both worlds,' Danielle corrected, surprised by

Zenaide's admission. Was she then mistaken in thinking Arab women to be completely beneath the domination of their men?

Apparently so. Zanaide made several enlightening comments as she washed and dried Danielle's hair, and a far different picture from what she had previously had began to emerge in Danielle's mind. As well as receiving schooling many of the brighter girls were encouraged to train abroad, and as long as the Muslim laws were observed and they were discreet women had a far greater degree of freedom than Danielle had envisaged.

'Of course we cannot go dancing and mix freely with the opposite sex in the European fashion,' Zanaide told her practically, 'but Sheikh Hassan has already done much for us, and promises to do more. Many of us prefer to wear the *chadrah* and retain our way of life,' she added softly. 'Is it not true that there often lies enticement in the unknown which the familiar does not possess? So it is with us, our very unavailability is enticing to our menfolk.'

The meal was over at last. Danielle made her escape thankfully. Everyone had been very kind, but the strain of trying to remember so many different names, on top of her long journey and strange surroundings, had all culminated in her feeling that all she really wanted to do was to go and lie down on her bed.

She seemed to have drunk innumerable small cups of strong black coffee and would no doubt have been obliged to drink even more had Zoe not noticed her predicament and tactfully indicated that she was to shake her cup to signal that

she did not want any more. Also the food, although
delicious, had been richer than what she was
accustomed to, and it was with a feeling of intense
relief that Danielle followed the corridor towards
the spiral staircase which led to her room, where
she suspected that Zanaide would be waiting for
her.

The stairs seemed to go on for ever, with far
more flights than she remembered, but telling
herself that it was just her imagination Danielle
picked up the heavy folds of her enveloping *chadrah* and wearily climbed upwards.

Wall sconces illuminated the stairwell, and in
the corners shadows flickered in the draught from
the open shutters. One of them even seemed to
move towards her, and Danielle bit back a startled
gasp as she realised that what she had mistaken
for a shadow was in fact a man clad in a dark
robe, which was nowhere near as enveloping as
her own because it had fallen open to disclose a
tanned chest, sprinkled with crisp dark hairs, still
damp from a shower or some similar activity, as
was the thick dark hair lying crisply over a skull
whose structure reminded her of the heads
depicted on ancient coins. The face beneath it was
arrestingly male, with high prominent cheekbones
set below eyes so dark that at first she thought
they were actually black until the man moved,
addressing some crisp words to her in what she
presumed to be Arabic, and she saw that his
eyes—eyes which were studying her with an arrogance that sent the hair prickling up on the back
of her neck—were actually very dark grey.

He spoke to her again, more sharply this time,
the words commanding.

'I . . . I . . . don't understand. I only speak English,' she faltered hesitantly, not sure that he would understand her.

His teeth flashed brilliant white in the darkness of his face, faint creases fanning out from his eyes and the sardonic curl of his lips. A sensation she had never experienced before curled insidiously through her lower stomach, making her clench her muscles and take an involuntary step backwards.

A lean hand grasped her wrist, cool mint-scented breath wafting past her ear as she was hauled unceremoniously forward.

'You were looking for me?'

His English was faultless, but the question held no hint of kindness; rather a suggestion of leashed power combined with cool impatience.

Danielle could only stare at him, mechanically rubbing the wrist he had grasped to prevent her from moving backwards.

'I was looking for my room.'

His dark eyebrows shot upwards in disbelief. 'In this part of the palace? Surely you must realise that these are not the women's quarters . . .'

It was the haughty tone of the words rather than their content which caused Danielle to flush guiltily and stare disbelievingly down the way she had come, stammering, 'Oh, but I know I took the right way . . .'

Her companion was plainly not impressed. His smile had disappeared, leaving a sternly autocratic expression in its place. How old was he? Danielle wondered. Thirty? Perhaps a little older? It was hard to tell in the half-light, but whatever his age there was no doubt that he was a man to be reckoned with. In spite of her immediate anti-

pathy towards him Danielle could not help but be
aware of his intense masculinity, of the spare,
narrow waist beneath the thin robe; the taut,
muscular thighs which the thin silk did little to
disguise.

'So . . .' His eyes seemed to burn past her
defences, ruthlessly removing them and reading
her mind with lazy ease. He knew exactly what
effect his presence was having upon her, Danielle
thought resentfully. She even suspected that he
could have gauged the rate of her heart and pulse
beats with exact accuracy. She turned away, unwilling for him to see the betraying quiver of her
lips, suddenly overwhelmed by an instinctive
desire to escape. Escape from what? she asked
herself crossly. Was she so susceptible to her surroundings that already she was behaving in the
presence of an unknown man as Zoe or Zanaide
might? What had happened to all her British
independence; all her determination to retain her
own personality?

Her chin lifted unconsciously.

'I did not realise that I had left the women's
quarters. If you would be kind enough to direct
me . . .'

She stiffened as she caught the white flash of
his teeth once more, convinced that he was laughing at her, but there was no laughter in the dark
eyes as they studied her features with lazy scrutiny.

'You are very daring,' he said softly. 'Or is it
merely ignorance which lures the dove to trespass
on the hawk's domain without asking what
penalty he may exact for that trespass?'

Tired and confused, Danielle stared mutely up

at him, gasping with shock when both arms came
out to grip her waist, propelling her forward until
her body was pressed against the alien male one,
his warm breath fanning her cheek as he bent his
head and without mercy took her lips in a kiss far
more intimate than any she had experienced
before, the hands at her waist, biting into her flesh
like steel pincers, holding her against a body
which she realised with icy shock was completely
naked beneath the brief robe.

That realisation restored some of her stunned
senses. She pushed fiercely against the solid wall
of muscle beneath her fingers, appalled by the
unwanted intimacy of her fingertips against the
hair-roughened flesh, but it was too late to withdraw. Her futile attempts to be free were stifled
with a cruel laugh and the immediate capture of
her protesting fists, her fingers uncurled and
placed fingertip to palm against the smoothly
muscled flesh, while the pillaging lips left hers
long enough to quirk mockingly and say softly,

'So . . . the British are not always as careless of
their women's virtue as we would believe. You
blush like the rose which blooms in the inner
courtyard,' the taunting voice continued. 'You too
are an enclosed courtyard . . . unknown and
undiscovered . . .'

'Stop it!' Danielle protested, at last finding her
voice. 'I won't listen to you! Let me go . . . I shall
complain to the Sheikha!'

His laughter completely unnerved her, but at
least she was released from that uncomfortably
intimate contact with his body, although his long
fingers still circled one slender wrist.

'Do that, *mignonne*,' he taunted softly. 'But first

do you not want to know whom you must complain of?'

Confused by his abrupt change of front, Danielle could only stare at him through the darkness, wondering a little at the prickly, warning sensation being relayed to her by her senses. What was the matter with her? she demanded of herself. Surely she hadn't gone so completely spineless that the presence of a mere man (and an arrogantly unpleasant one at that) had the power to overwhelm her like this?

She glanced upwards uncertainly at the dark, chiselled features, noting instinctively the autocratic curl of the long mouth and the taut line of a jaw which she sensed could clench frighteningly in anger, but which was now relaxed in lazy amusement.

'What, nothing to say?' the soft voice taunted.

The lean fingers moved from her wrists to her shoulders, tracing the shape of her through the double thickness of her robe and her caftan with a sure knowledge that made her clench her teeth against her frantic protest. This was a man who knew women, and he was playing with her, enjoying her anguished embarrassment. Sparks flew from her eyes and she stiffened automatically, but he only laughed again, a low, warm chuckle which infuriated her more than everything that had gone before, one hand hovering tauntingly over her breast without actually touching her flesh until both of them could hear the nervous shallowness of her breath.

'Your heart sings under my hand like a trapped bird,' he said softly, placing palm and fingers against that organ.

Danielle stepped back as though she had been burned, and indeed the warmth generated by his hand against her body was such that she wouldn't have been surprised to discover that it had actually scorched her flesh, but his grip of her shoulder prevented her from moving very far.

With lazy appreciation his hand was removed from her now fast beating heart, to push back the hood of her robe and reveal the tumbled disorder of the curls Zanaide had so carefully brushed before the evening meal. The thin light from the wall sconce turned her hair to living fire, and Danielle gasped as the soft voice drawled with a thread of living steel,

'Well met by candlelight, daughter of Hassan.'

It should have sounded ridiculous, and in any other circumstances it might well have done so, but here in this ancient palace fortress, surrounded by strangers, Danielle could only react after the fashions she had always despised in novel heroines, by demanding breathlessly,

'Who are you?'

He moved fractionally and in the faint light she could see the sardonic lift of his eyebrows, the smile that twisted his lips with bitterness and never reached his eyes; the powerful thrust of his body, which almost seemed to menace her as they stood together a frozen tableau in a world in which no other human beings might have existed.

'You mean you honestly don't know?'

His abrupt change of front, from laconic mockery to ice-cold hauteur, frightened Danielle. The air around her seemed to grow colder, filled with some malevolent presence.

'How could I know?' Danielle found herself stammering nervously. 'I have only just arrived, I . . .'

'So have I, and finding you on your way to my private apartments made me think that you must have some pressing purpose in seeking me out. A logical conclusion, would you not say, daughter of Hassan? You see, I know much of your race. The British are addicted to logic, are they not?'

'Well, you're wrong,' Danielle said hotly, ignoring the latter part of his speech to deny his claim that she had been looking for him—or for anyone, for that matter. 'I was on my way to my own apartment. I must have taken a wrong turning . . .'

Now, too late, she remembered how the stairs had seemed to go on for ever. If only she had stopped then and retraced her steps! 'Besides, what possible motive could I have for seeking you out?'

She was pleased with the amount of scorn she managed to inject into the words, but her pleasure was soon swamped by another emotion as she witnessed the sudden tightening of the lean jaw. As she had suspected, it denoted anger; an anger which was soon unleashed about her, inducing the dry-mouthed terror of a sudden storm as he said with a softness which menaced where it had earlier mocked,

'A very strong one, I should have thought, daughter of Hassan. I am Jourdan Saud Ibn Ahmed.'

CHAPTER FOUR

WAS it her imagination or had the earth really moved under her feet? Danielle thought weakly, her mind a frantic jumble of thoughts as she sought to come to terms with what she had just been told.

'But you're supposed to be in France,' she protested. 'I . . .'

'You would never have come had you thought otherwise?' he said for her. 'How little you know of men, daughter of Hassan, for all your modern upbringing. Did you honestly think I would allow you to insult me in such a fashion? To refuse me as your husband?'

Cruel fingers gripped her wrists like the talons of the eagle her stepfather claimed he represented. A terrible cold fear gripped Danielle in a numbing embrace. She couldn't believe that this was happening. She would have to return home immediately; she would phone her parents. But they were in America, travelling from coast to coast in a hectic round of business and social commitments. The Sheikha, then, Danielle decided, her thoughts leaping the chasm of her fear. She would surely help her. If only she had insisted on her stepfather providing her with some money! She would have no need of any, he had told her calmly. Indeed her hosts would think it an insult if she tried to use any. But surely her air fare home, she had protested, but again her protest had been swept aside. She would be travelling in the family jet; a luxury which would not be bought simply by queueing up at an airline desk and purchasing a ticket.

Round and round went her thoughts until Danielle was dizzy with the effort of containing them, and all the time the man standing only feet away from her in the shadows retained his biting grip of her wrist.

'I shall not apologise to you,' she said swiftly, colour burning her face as anger came to her rescue. 'I've done nothing to apologise for.'

He was more astute than she had bargained for, for instead of letting the matter drop, he enquired with dangerous calm.

'Meaning?'

When Danielle remained stubbornly silent, he goaded softly, 'So, the daughter of Hassan lacks the courage she would lay claim to. It is very easy to scatter insults in the heat of the moment, *mignonne*, but far harder to justify them.'

'Meaning that any man who marries a girl purely for financial gain, as a business undertaking, has everything to apologise for!' Danielle burst out furiously. 'I disliked what I heard about you before I knew what you and my stepfather had planned between you, but after that . . .'

'What did you hear about me?' Jourdan demanded, his eyes narrowing sharply. He was like a panther, Danielle thought fearfully, tensed and waiting, coiled to spring upon her fragile arguments and rend and scatter them to the winds. 'And where?'

'From a friend of mine,' Danielle responded, refusing to be quelled, her chin firming courage-ously. 'Philippe Sancerre.' Her upper lip curled faintly. 'I suppose I should consider myself fortunate. All I would have been forced to bear was your name, while other women are obliged to endure your possession of them without even the saving grace of that.'

For a moment she thought he meant to strike her. She stepped back instinctively, appalled by the fierce glitter in the now almost black eyes.

'Think yourself fortunate that I realise that your insults are those of a child who knows not what she is saying,' Jourdan told her grimly, adding with a cold sneer, 'A child, who betrays her very youth in her speech.' He leaned a little closer to her, his warm breath grazing her temple. 'A child, who knows nothing concerning that of which she speaks so disparagingly.' His eyes swept Danielle's now shivering form. 'So you think my possession is to be endured, do you, *mignonne*? You shrink from me in horror and disgust? And you talk of a marriage where all you would be required to bear would be my name. Think again, little fool, and so that you may have something to think about . . .' He bent his head, at the same time drawing her towards him, his fingers leaving her wrist to grip her shoulder while his free hand tilted her face upward until she was blinking protestingly as the light from the wall sconce fell fully on to her startled features.

'You are as timid as the gazelle that grazes by the oases,' he mocked softly. 'Your eyes are those of a timid, hunted creature. Where is your bravery now, daughter of Hassan? Am I not only a man— only flesh and blood, whose heart beats even as yours does. Can't you feel it beneath your fingers?'

Her hand was trapped and spread against the warmth of the flesh beneath the thin gown. She prayed desperately that someone would come and rescue her from this nightmare situation, and as though he read her thoughts Jourdan said sardonically, 'No one will come to rescue you. These are my private quarters. Think upon this, daughter of Hassan. Should I choose to show you exactly what it means to know my possession there is none to gainsay me; none to overhear your timid virgin cries . . .'

'I am not a vir . . .' Danielle began, but he swept aside her words with a husky laugh.

'You lie, Danielle. If it were otherwise you would know without my having to tell you that a man finds piquantly attractive the thought of a girl whose body is as the most perfectly concealed courtyard. Indeed, I am surprised that Sancerre has not already told you this.'

'What makes you think he hasn't?' Danielle retorted, wishing she had the courage to press harder against the hard warm chest beneath her splayed fingers, and thus free herself, although, of course, whatever puny effort she might make to escape would be swiftly quelled by the iron-hard arm circling her waist.

'Because had he done so, he would not merely have told you in words,' was the calm reply. 'And your fingers would not tremble so timidly against my flesh, nor your eyes widen with fear of the unknown when I touch you thus . . .'

Danielle gasped and stiffened as her robe was pushed carelessly aside and lean fingers cupped her breast. Beneath the caftan she was wearing only tiny lacy briefs, having been persuaded by Zanaide that her taut youthful breasts needed no extra support.

Her heart hammering like a drum, she felt her mouth go dry, her frantic thoughts protesting that this could not be happening, that this careless, arrogant stranger could not be sweeping aside all her defences and caressing her breast in this intimate fashion.

'How young you are! And how foolish.' Jourdan's voice seemed to have deepened, his touch mockingly sure as the tiny loops fastening the front of the caftan were released, and Danielle's panicky protest was lost beneath the pressure of his mouth as it descended to hover threateningly over hers before its cool mastery was forcing her stunned senses to assimilate emotions and sensations completely outside all her existing experience.

Beneath his tormenting fingers she felt her breast swell and harden, her mouth parting irresistibly for the demanding insistence of his tongue as it slid moistly over her lips, her whole body becoming pliant with a sensation that made her feel as though she were unable to do anything but give in to the strange power he seemed to have over her.

When his mouth left hers sanity returned and she tried to push away from him, but his lips were sliding from her throat downwards, his voice husky with mingled mockery and laughter as he murmured.

'Be still, daughter of Hassan, lest I take your inexperienced squirming for a plea to know that complete possession of which you are at once so innocent and so scathing.'

'Let me go!' Danielle demanded breathlessly, conscious of hurried breathing and thumping heart, but Jourdan ignored her, his lips continuing their downward path until they came to rest for a heart-stopping moment against the smooth curve of her breast. Shocked, Danielle froze, only to gasp and tremble as his fingers curved warmly against her breast and his mouth closed over the tender pinkness of her nipple, savouring its burgeoning arousal and encouraging it until Danielle felt weak with the throbbing pressure of her own body, and horrified by the overwhelming sensation of pleasure radiating all over her body from the place where his mouth was caressing her flesh.

When he moved and straightened she all but collapsed, and would have fallen had his arms not come round her with lazy amusement.

'What has shocked you the most?' he asked her laconically, casually fastening her robe. 'What I did or how you felt?'

'I felt nothing,' Danielle lied vigorously. 'Unless you count my revulsion . . .'

'Revulsion?'

For one hideous horror-filled moment Danielle thought he wasn't going to release her, but then to her relief he stepped backwards, his hair gleaming under the light, his eyes brilliant with sardonic amusement.

'Oh no, little one, I can't be challenged in that fashion, and besides, I am too tired to begin the initiation of a virgin tonight, although I confess it would be intriguing to lie with you in my arms on a bed of satin cushions and remove the layers of prudery and pride with which you think you have so successfuly protected yourself.

'Come, show me that you are not such a child as you appear, and admit that my touch was not . . . unpleasant . . .'

'Unpleasant? Oh no, it was not unpleasant,' Danielle gritted, fear and anger igniting to push her beyond the bounds of caution. 'Rather it was degrading, insulting, revolting and totally and completely repulsive!' she stormed at him, turning tail and running back down the stairs before he could reach out for her.

At the bottom of the first flight she paused to get her breath, listening for the sound of him behind her, but only silence had followed her.

She descended two more flights at a more decorous pace, and then discovered where she had originally gone wrong.

Zanaide was waiting for her in her room.

'The Sitt is late,' she began anxiously, but Danielle silenced her, explaining that she had got lost.

'I thought Jourdan was in France,' she added.

'The Sheikh has returned this very evening,' Zanaide told her, paling a little as she eyed Danielle's flushed face. 'The Sitt did not take the staircase to the Sheikh's private quarters in error?'

'Unfortunately, yes,' Danielle admitted dryly.

What had happened to her on the stairs refused to be banished to the far recesses of her mind; her heart was still thundering and her breast still throbbed betrayingly, but she wasn't going to discuss with anyone else what had occurred, even someone as sympathetic as Zanaide.

'The Sheikh Jourdan is very handsome,'

Zanaide confounded her by saying, 'and very much a man. To lie with him would surely bring great pleasure. He is not of our faith and for this reason must only take one wife. Many of the Sheikha's family wish that he would choose from amongst their daughters, for he is powerful and wealthy . . .'

'He is arrogant and domineering,' Danielle said through gritted teeth, 'and I don't want to hear one more word about him.'

'The Sitt does not find him attractive?' Zanaide asked, plainly puzzled.

'About as attractive as a snake,' Danielle muttered as Zanaide helped her off with her caftan. 'And twice as dangerous!'

When Zanaide had gone and she was alone in her room, compelled by some strange inner prompting Danielle slid out of bed and moved like a sleepwalker to the mirror-lined dressing room, where she slowly stepped out of her night-dress and studied the pale, glimmering shape of her naked body, one hand going instinctively to cup the swelling breast which was somehow no longer completely part of her, but seemed to have developed an alien life of its own, a life summoned into being by Jourdan's knowing touch. A sound suspiciously like a sob broke the silence of the room. Danielle reached frenziedly for her night-gown, unable to bear the sight of her naked flesh and know how it had betrayed her, willing herself not to remember with such vivid clarity exactly how it had felt to have Jourdan's lips tease her nipple into erect obedience and the pleasure which had followed.

CHAPTER FIVE

THE following day was so busy that Danielle wasn't given the opportunity to brood. As soon as she had breakfasted on fresh rolls, honey and hot sweet coffee she was hurried downstairs by Zanaide and out into a large courtyard where a large black Rolls purred softly in tune to the gentle fall of water from a fountain into a basin.

A white chauffeur wearing a dishdash opened the door for her and Danielle slid obediently inside, to sit next to the Sheikha, who greeted her with a kind smile.

'You slept well, daughter of Hassan?' she asked.

Danielle nodded wishing she could pluck up the courage to ask the Sheikha to call her by her own name; 'daughter of Hassan' roused too many memories she would rather leave sleeping, and she could feel her body tensing as they surfaced.

'It is the normal practice for the silk merchants to visit the palace when we choose new clothes,' the Sheikha explained. 'They normally come once a month—an occasion of great excitement for my household, when everyone gathers in the audience room. My daughters-in-law join us also with their households, and we spend the day choosing fabric and drinking coffee.'

'It sounds fun,' Danielle murmured politely, but it was obvious that she had not deceived the Sheikha, because the older woman gave her a

shrewd glance, and signalled to the driver to close
the panel which separated the driver and escort
seated in the front of the Rolls from the Sheikha
and Danielle in the back.

'When women live as we do, we must make our
own pleasures,' the Sheikha said firmly. 'And you
must not despise us for those pleasures, Danielle.
My daughters-in-law all have university degrees;
all are fluent in English and French, and all run
large households, but it is the rule of our religion
that the sexes may not mingle freely, and a rule to
which we adhere.' Her face relaxed a fraction and
the smile she gave Danielle was comprehensive
and understanding. 'It sounds harsh to you, I
know, but it is less so than it seems. My husband,
although not as forward-thinking as Hassan, does
permit us to have lectures and slides on topical
subjects, to that we are all well versed on inter-
national matters. We have stimulating debates for
those of us who wish to sharpen the mind, and if
all these pleasures are restricted purely to our own
sex, is it not really a little hypocritical of
Europeans to take less pleasure in them for that,
for surely if stimulating company and discussion
is the sole object of debate and discussion, it is an
insult to one's own sex to presume that their
company is less pleasurable than that of a man.'

The Sheikha was a skilled debator, Danielle
acknowledged. And in essence what she had said
was quite true, However, what she objected to
most was not the lack of male company, but the
lack of free choice.

When she said as much to her companion, the
Sheikha shook her head and smiled.

'You think this is so, but it is not. One may

have the company of one's husband, or one's father . . .'

'But only at their discretion,' Danielle said bitterly.

The Sheikha's eyebrows rose.

'And you think it beyond a woman's powers to ensure that a man—especially her husband—enjoys her company; treasures the precious moments he may spend with her like an oyster guarding pearls. Shame on you, Danielle! Your Woman's Lib has robbed you Europeans of your faith in your own ability to attract and hold, something which our girls know almost from the cradle. A woman can make her husband's life heaven or hell if she chooses; a wise women chooses to make it heaven, for when there is harmony in the home there is happiness in the heart. You underestimate your own sex, I think, Danielle,' the Sheikha concluded. 'Do you not have a saying, "The hand that rocks the cradle rules the world"? Think upon the truth of those words.

'Now,' she said briskly, changing the subject, 'Kadir will drive us down al Muhammad Street, so that you might see the new buildings our family is erecting. There is the new library,' she announced, pointing out a gleaming new building, built on Eastern lines and extremely attractive. 'And next to it the medical college and the hospital. Hassan has told my husband that we must educate our sons for the day when oil will no longer reign supreme, and to this end many new industries and technologies are being developed, but these are all concentrated in an area several miles away from the capital. Later we shall take you to see the other side of the town which lies along the coast. Beyond it are beaches and a small island which used to be the centre of our pearl industry.'

'Do men still dive for pearls?' Danielle asked, intrigued.

'A few, but they are mainly Europeans,' the Sheikha replied with a certain amount of dry humour. 'It is a dangerous occupation and a brief one, and unless one finds pearls of perfect colour and shape a poorly rewarded one.'

Their driver turned off the main arterial highway and down another dual carriageway with a centre aisle planted with flowering shrubs and discreetly placed street lights from which hung flowering baskets.

'You are admiring our flowers,' the Sheikha commented. 'They are indeed a pleasure to all of us, especially those of us who can remember when all this was arid desert. It is the work of my brother,' she added proudly. 'With Hassan's encouragement he has built a large desalination plant which provides water for the growing of food, and enough surplus to permit us to grow grass, trees and flowers in our city. Truly to the Arab there is no more miraculous sight than those, growing where once there was only sand. It is a mark of how far we have progressed that our children merely accept this miracle without wonder.'

Either side of the road stretched impressively façaded shops filled with a mouthwatering assortment of goods, especially jewellery, but it was in front of a discreet, small establishment up a narrow street that the Rolls eventually stopped.

Their escort was in uniform and armed, and

Danielle shuddered when she saw his gun.

'It is better to be safe than sorry,' the Sheikha told her gently, seeing her expression. 'These are dangerous times in the Middle East. Qu'Har is a very small and a very rich country, without a strong guiding hand on the reins it could all too easily be torn apart by our powerful neighbours, should they so desire. But today is not the day for serious discussion,' she added, smiling again. 'To do so will cloud the colours of the silks, and spoil their beauty.'

To Danielle's relief the guard remained outside while they entered the shop. To Danielle's surprise, a woman came forward to attend to them, nothing servile about her as she prostrated herself before the Sheikha and then rose with one lithe, swift movement.

Danielle gasped when she saw her face. She was one of the most beautiful women she had ever seen, her complexion flawless.

'Zara, this is Danielle, daughter of Hassan,' the Sheikha said by way of introduction. 'Danielle, Zara is my cousin, and what you would perhaps call a career woman, is this not so, Zara?' she appealed, obviously enjoying Danielle's patent astonishment.

Zara laughed.

'My cousin the Sheikha teases you a little, I think, Danielle. It is true that my father permits me to buy silks and run this shop, although of course I only attend the ladies of the palace . . . I am fortunate in having such a generous and understanding family,' Zara continued on a more serious note, 'for otherwise I must surely have lost my senses. My husband was killed in an explosion at the oilfield a week after we were married. I was eighteen,' she told Danielle briefly, her eyes clouding. 'As I had no children to comfort me, no will to live without my husband whom I had loved since we were children, Jourdan suggested I start this business. I believe his suggestion saved my sanity and my life. He is a very generous and understanding man.'

'And also a very attractive one,' the Sheikha said, so wryly that for a moment Danielle's heart almost stopped beating. Jourdan was all male animal; she knew that, and Zara was an extremely beautiful woman. Could she be his mistress? Or should she say, one of his mistresses?

She wasn't given time to dwell on the matter. Zara gave a brief command in Arabic and two girls appeared carrying bales of silk which were placed on the low table surrounded by silk cushions.

'Please sit down, Danielle,' Zara offered. 'One of my girls will bring us coffee and then we shall settle down to the serious business of choosing silks.'

'Do you require anything my cousin?' she asked the Sheikha, who shook her head. Danielle envied the way the other two women could sit so comfortably cross-legged, while her muscles protested violently at the position, and she knew she looked nowhere near as elegant and relaxed as her two companions.

A shy young maid brought coffee which they drank, while more bales of silk were brought to the table and when, and only when the coffee cups were removed did Zara assume her business manner and start describing the silks, pointing out those she considered most suitable for Danielle.

'The green with the gold embroidery, and the bronze . . . There is also an amber, a good shade for one of your colouring, and of course yellow.'

In the end the Sheikha insisted on purchasing half a dozen different silks for Danielle, which she told her would be made up by the palace dressmakers.

'Many of our women now prefer to buy their clothes in Paris and New York, but personally I think there is nothing quite as flattering as the caftan.'

'It is very exotic.' Danielle admitted, fingering a bolt of pretty turquoise silk embroidered with tiny crystal beads. 'But I should be very reluctant to put away my jeans for ever.'

'We have yet to purchase perfume for you, and shoes,' the Sheikha announced when they had taken their leave of Zara. 'The shoes will be made especially for you at the palace, but perfume blending is an art best left to the experts, and we must visit the suk another day for that. We of the East are great believers in the value of perfumes. Correctly used they can greatly influence the senses, more than you may imagine. You have a saying amongst the men of your country, "At night all cats are grey." Is this not so? However, in our country it is believed that a woman expresses herself as much by her perfume as her personality and that because of it she is instantly recognisable to those who know her even clad in her robe on the darkest night. We take pride in wearing our scent, knowing it to be an important way of expressing ourselves.'

On their return to the palace Danielle was

tempted outside into the courtyards she had been
told were specifically for the women. After
making sure she was wearing an adequate amount
of barrier cream and having declined Zanaide's
offer to accompany her she went out into the
courtyard, walking at first beneath the shady
clumps of palms and along the bougainvillea-
smothered cloisters before venturing out between
the intricately paved paths to sit by one of the
many ornamental ponds and watch the multi-
coloured carp basking by the lily pads. The
courtyard was an oasis of peace in what was obviously a busy household, and Danielle had it to
herself. No expense had been spared in its con-
struction, and each direction one looked delighted
the eye with fresh pleasures. Tiny humming birds
darted in and out of the creepers, moving so fast
that one only had to blink to miss them; doves
cooed softly in the background and the strident
call of a peacock somewhere in the distance barely
disturbed the drowsy peace of the afternoon.

Danielle sat back and closed her eyes, but the
minute she did so the image of a mocking dark
face imprinted itself behind her eyes and she had
to open them again. She would not think of
Jourdan, she told herself firmly, walking aimlessly
down one of the paths which terminated at a
heavy wooden door set into the wall.

Memories of reading *The Secret Garden* enticed
her to turn the iron handle.

Beyond the door was another courtyard around
which were arranged horseboxes, velvety muzzles
stretched over half open doors. As Danielle stood
wondering whether to go or stay, a familiar figure
came towards her, and she forgot Zanaide's warn-

ing lessons and she hurried towards him, her face breaking into a pleased smile.

'Saud!'

He blushed a little but took her hands and held them firmly, his eyes alight with pleasure.

'What are you doing here?' Danielle asked him. She had never met him before he escorted her to Qu'Har, but now he seemed like an old friend.

'The Sheikh wishes to ride and I am come to instruct the men to saddle his stallion,' he replied, indicating the glossy black Arab stallion which was being led into the courtyard. The animal's coat gleamed like silk, the small ears twitching a little intimidatingly as he minced delicately over the stones.

'He comes from a long line of stallions bred only for our Royal Family. Only they are allowed to mount such animals, and in days gone by it used to be considered a test of a young sheikh's manhood to see if he could mount and ride one of these animals. Although the test is no longer applied, there is still much honour to the man who can ride and control such an animal.'

Danielle could well believe it. It was taking two grooms to hold the stallion, who was pawing the ground and snorting resentfully as they held grimly on to the reins.

'You are enjoying your stay in our country?' Saud asked Danielle. 'I hear from my sister that you have this morning been shopping.'

'Your sister?'

'Zoe,' he explained with a smile, suddenly biting his lip and glancing cautiously over his shoulder. 'Forgive me, Miss Danielle, but you should not be here, nor talking to me like this. I tell you for your own sake, not mine,' he added earnestly, his eyes suddenly warm as they rested on Danielle's soft mouth. 'For myself there is nothing I would rather do than be here with you, unless it were perhaps to walk in the velvet darkness of the oasis with you, just the two of us beneath a new moon . . .'

'But, Saud, you are betrothed,' Danielle reminded him, suddenly feeing that the conversation had got out of hand.

Before he could reply a deeply authoritative voice called abruptly.

'Saud, where is my mount?' and Danielle's heart dropped as she saw coming towards her, dressed in riding breeches, a falcon resting on one leather-gauntleted hand, the man whose image had pursued her in her nightmares, and whose presence now made the blood drain from her face, and a weak desire to turn and run engulfed her.

Saud, for his part, looked as guilty as a small child caught out in some forbidden misdemeanour, the look he gave Danielle at once apologetic and full of fear.

Jourdan, on the other hand, looked completely relaxed and in control. One hand held the reins of the prancing stallion, the other transferred the hooded falcon to a waiting servant before turning to coolly survey Danielle and Saud, for all the world as though they were a pair of miscreants caught out in some dreadful crime, Danielle thought wrathfully, deliberately closing her mind to the tiny voice telling her that Jourdan's expression held undertones of an anger kept strictly in check, but still dangerously close to the surface.

'Saud, I shall speak to you later,' Jourdan announced crisply, watching the younger man crimson at his tone, without a hint of compassion. There was something cruel about the way his lips curled faintly, Danielle thought, her heart beating hurriedly as he turned from Saud, suddenly crestfallen and very, very young, to study her flushed cheeks and defiant eyes.

'It is my fault, not Saud's,' Danielle told him imperiously, her words ringing out across the yard, and causing a couple of the grooms to glance curiously in her direction.

'I came here by mistake, and he was just telling me so.'

'You seem to have a habit of doing things "by mistake", daughter of Hassan,' Jourdan said with heavy irony, 'You leap to my young cousin's defence like the lioness defending her cub . . . why?'

The word cut into her like a lash, but Danielle still stood her ground.

'Primarily because I hate to see anyone bullied,' she retorted promptly, 'and secondly because I happen to be very fond of Saud.'

An electric silence followed her uncompromising statement. Saud's face lit up as though illuminated from within, and Danielle immediately regretted her words, seeing that Saud had read into them a meaning she had never meant to convey—and Jourdan? She glanced sideways at the impassively handsome face. There was nothing to be read there, only a certain dangerous glint in the eyes which were studying her, faintly narrowed against the harsh glare of the sun, the mouth pulled down at the corners.

'Go back to the women's quarters, daughter of Hassan,' Jourdan ordered abruptly, 'and try to remember that my cousin is a betrothed man. Besides,' he added, casually turning to mount the stallion, and holding him in with iron control while he walked him to Danielle's side, to stare down into her upturned face with cool scrutiny. 'If you wish to experiment, *mignonne*, you would be wiser choosing a man if not older, then at least . . . wiser.'

Without a backward glance he was gone, the stallion's hooves thudding in time to Danielle's swiftly beating heart.

Quite why she remained where she was staring after the unyielding retreating back she could not have said, but at last she roused herself as though from a trance, and hurried back the way she had come to the tranquillity of the Sheikha's garden.

It was later in the afternoon, when Danielle was resting in her room, and avoiding the full heat of the day, that she had a summons from the Sheikha to attend her to be measured for her new clothes.

'The girl will measure you and then the caftans will be made up for you,' the Sheikha told Danielle.

While the shy young girl was carefully sliding a tape round her slim hips Danielle heard the dressmaker say something to the Sheikha.

'Naomi says that you are as slender as the young fig tree before it bears fruit,' the Sheikha said to Danielle. 'She is also to make Zoe's wedding gown. It is the tradition for the women of my husband's family to be married in crimson silk and the one hundred and one buttons closing the caftan to be of pearl. Zoe's robe will be embroidered with the emblems of fertility and her husband-to-be will give her the silver girdle which after the ceremony only he will have the right to unfasten.'

Bondage in more ways than one, Danielle told herself. But for some reason, it was not Zoe's pale face she saw rising from a mist of crimson silk, as lean, dark hands that reached arrogantly for the silver girdle, but her own, her eyes strained and nervous as she stared upwards at the man towering above.

'You have been standing for too long,' the Sheikha anounced, breaking Danielle's reverie. 'I have arranged that this afternoon you will be shown the coastline which stretches from the town east and west. The drive will do you good. Zanaide will accompany you.'

Thus dismissed, Danielle thanked the dressmaker and her assistants and hurried back to her own room, where she found Zanaide waiting for her, one of the pretty silk suits she had brought with her already lying carefully on her bed.

Danielle frowned a little when she saw it. The silk was pretty but creased easily, and she had planned to wear something a little more casual as they were simply going for a drive, but Zanaide was already hurrying into the bathroom, and rather than hurt the girl's feelings by ignoring the clothes she had so painstakingly laid out, Danielle slipped off her skirt and blouse and padded over to the dressing room to find clean briefs and bra.

She hadn't intended to do more than have a quick wash, but once again Zanaide had other ideas, and as Danielle stepped out of the dressing room, the scent of sandalwood enveloped her in its heavy sweetness.

'I don't want a bath, Zanaide,' she protested, but the girl looked so perturbed and upset that Danielle was forced to relent and step into the warm perfumed water.

Had someone told her three days ago that she would be lying full length in a marble bath almost deep enough to swim in, actually enjoying having someone gently massage perfumed oils into her skin, and bathing her, she would have laughed outright, but there was something so soporific about being thus shamelessly indulged that it was too much of an effort to resist, never mind protest.

Dried and perfumed, Danielle stepped into brief silk underwear and the silk suit Zanaide had put out for her.

It was a rich golden yellow, the shade of mellow buttercups and Danielle knew that the colour emphasised the dark, living russet of her hair, and the pure unclouded green of her eyes. A touch of soft beige and green eyeshadow, the merest suggestion of lipstick, and the reflection staring back at her from the mirror was all at once that of a woman and not an adolescent. Caught off guard, Danielle stared at herself, as though at a stranger. Had her mouth always had that tremulous fullness? Had her eyes always been so mysteriously shadowed and secret? It must surely be a trick of the light?

The car was waiting for them—not the Rolls this time, but a discreetly opulent BMW. Zanaide slid quietly into the front next to the driver. A servant opened the rear door for Danielle to get into the back. She was in, the door closed, and the car gliding smoothly away before she realised that she wasn't alone in the back of the car.

'You look pale, daughter of Hassan,' the smooth male voice mocked.

'Jourdan!' Danielle whispered the name through shocked lips. 'What are you doing here?'

She felt rather than saw the broad shoulders lift. 'Why should I not be? The Sheikha requested me to escort you, and here I am.'

Despite the perfectly logical explanation Danielle felt curiously uneasy. Jourdan had not struck her as a man to tamely accept the orders of another, especially a woman, even though that woman was the wife of the ruler of Qu'Har.

'Perhaps you would have preferred me to be Saud?' the smooth voice mocked unkindly. 'It seems you have quite a disastrous effect on impressionable young men, daughter of Hassan.'

'All we were doing was talking,' Danielle protested angrily. 'It was completely innocent.'

'There is no such thing as innocence between a man and a woman,' Danielle was told arrogantly, 'and to imply that there can be shows how little you know of the world, *mignonne*, or how competent you are at deceiving yourself.'

Rather than listen to his taunts any longer, Danielle stared deliberately through the window. She could just see the sweeping blue-green shimmer of the gulf beyond gardens sheltered with clusters of palms, but as she watched the coastline seemed to recede rather than draw nearer, and she frowned as she looked ahead and saw that the dual carriageway they were travelling was taking them away from the coast rather than closer to it.

They came to an intersection and she waited for them to turn towards the gulf, but instead the car moved swiftly in completely the opposite direction, through what were obviously the suburbs of the town, dotted with expensive villas, which grew sparser in inverse proportion to the empty acres of sand. Concerned, Danielle glanced over her shoulder. They had come several miles out of the town. Where were they going?

She voiced the question sharply, and for her pains received only a taunting command to, 'wait and see.'

Anxiety changed to fear. Danielle turned sharply in her seat, staring at the retreating city. Where was she being taken? She looked wildly towards the driver, intending to demand that he stop the car instantly, then she remembered that Zanaide was seated in front with him and her fear dissolved a little. Jourdan was playing with her. He had deliberately fostered her alarm. She wished she hadn't let him see how well he had succeeded.

She sat in silence as they travelled further and further into the desert. It was a battle of wills, Danielle told herself grimly, and one she had no intention of losing. They had been travelling for nearly an hour and the signs of human habitation they had passed had been a cluster of tents round a small oasis. They were probably travelling in a huge circle, Danielle reassured herself, trying not to feel overwhelmed by the vastness of the desert which now surrounded them. Sandhill succeeded sandhill; the sun was starting to dip down to the west, a crimson ball of fire, turning the sand the colour of blood. Danielle's head ached despite the car's luxurious uholstery and air-conditioning.

At last, when she could bear it no longer, she drew a painful breath and said shakily.

'You have had your fun, Jourdan, and I'm properly impressed, but surely we must be nearing the palace now? The Sheikha will be expecting us?'

'Right and wrong,' Jourdan replied laconically, 'We are nearing the palace, daughter of Hassan, but not that of my uncle the Sheikh.'

Even as he spoke a building appeared on the horizon, a wall, crenellated and set with huge wooden doors such as Danielle had seen in films. As they approached these swung open, swallowing them like a giant maw, she thought apprehensively, wondering why Zanaide made no protest.

Beyond the outer wall was a courtyard, shady with palm trees and clumps of flowers, two lions couchant in pale marble guarding the steps to the main doorway to the palace. The car came to rest exactly between the lions and Danielle reached for the door.

'You must wait until I precede you,' Jourdan told her calmly, his fingers gripping hers hard, and warm. 'Otherwise my people will think I do not have the respect of my wife . . .'

'Your wife?' Danielle gasped disbelievingly. A combination of heat and shock was making her feel dizzy, so dizzy that she could not protest as Zanaide helped her from the car out into the blood red rays of the dying sun, and from there to the cool shadows of a hallway tiled with mosaics and filled with the sound of the water which rose from a fountain and fell back into a bowl of rose quartz banded with gold.

'But I'm not your wife, Jourdan,' Danielle managed to stammer.

He stopped and turned, surveying her arrogantly from the advantage of his extra height, and Danielle shivered with a feeling which had nothing to do with the sudden change of temperature.

'Not yet, daughter of Hassan,' Jourdan agreed blandly. 'But before dawn you will be.'

CHAPTER SIX

WHERE was she? Danielle wondered muzzily, lifting her head from a pillow whose scent reminded her poignantly of her childhood. It was several seconds before she identified the scent as lavender, and during that time she realised that she was not in her bedroom at the palace of Qu'Har, but in a room which seemed to enbody all her imaginings of Eastern splendour.

Rich silks hung from the walls and curtained the windows; soft Persian rugs covered the cool marble floor, a bed which seemed to dwarf her tiny frame dominating the room, the draperies enclosing it all the myriad colours and shades of mother of pearl, and suspended from a gold circlet in the ceiling.

Even her clothes were different. Surely she had not come here wearing these flimsy silk underthings and nothing else? And then she remembered.

The door, which she now dimly remembered closing behind her with a decisive click, was locked. Her room—her prison, Danielle told herself bitterly—was round. Off it she discovered a luxurious bathroom, but nothing else.

She would not give way to tears, she told herself, biting her lip and curling her fingers into angry fists. Jourdan had no right to bring her here, no right to intimate that he meant to marry her. She would complain to the Sheikha and

demand to be allowed to return home straight
away. What would her stepfather think of his precious nephew when he learned of this outrage?
Not much.

Danielle was so engrossed in her thoughts that
she didn't see the door open and wasn't aware
that she was no longer alone until she caught sight
of Zanaide's apologetic expression in the mirror.

'Zanaide, what's going on?' she demanded,
relieved to see at least one friendly face. 'We must
leave here and return to Qu'Har!'

The little maid shook her head.

'It is not possible. The Sheikh has commanded
me to prepare the Sitt for her wedding. All is
arranged, even the priest of your religion is here.'

'Zanaide—you don't understand. I don't want
to marry the Sheikh. He only wants to marry me
for . . . for spite! Somehow you must find a way
of telling the Sheikha what has happened, she
will . . .'

Danielle broke off as Zaiade shook her head
firmly.

'No, Sitt. The Sheikha she tells me that you
are to be married. I have your wedding gown here
with me. It is fitting and right that you should be
nervous,' she added kindly. 'Marriage is a big step
for a woman, but with the Sheikh you will find
much pleasure,' she added slyly.

Danielle could only stare at her. The Sheikha
had told Zanaide that she was to marry Jourdan?
Her mouth compressed.

'I am not going to make a single move from
this bed until I've spoken to the Sheikh,' Danielle
announced determinedly.

'Intrepid, if somewhat foolish of you, *mig-*

nonne,' a new voice drawled from the open doorway. 'I wish to speak with your mistress,' Jourdan told Zanaide. 'You will leave us for a few minutes, and then return to prepare her for the ceremony.'

'What ceremony? There will not be one,' Danielle announced when Zanaide had gone. 'Have you gone mad, Jourdan?'

'Do I look as though I have?'

He had moved so silently that Danielle hadn't heard him, and now he was standing by the bed, glancing assessingly through the flimsy bed hangings to where Danielle sat defiantly on the silken cushions. She had forgotten until that moment that Zanaide had removed her silk suit and that she was wearing merely her briefs and bra. Shyness made her long to cover her exposed body, but pride burned fiercely inside her, forcing her to remain still beneath the probing look.

'I am making it easy for you, *mignonne*,' Jourdan said softly. 'I could make it so that you would be glad to marry me.'

'By taking my virginity?' Danielle said scornfully. 'You are behind the times, *monsieur*. Such things are of no importance these days . . .'

She heard the angry hiss as he expelled his breath and wrenched aside the semi-transparent draperies to stare down at her with eyes which seemed to strip the remaining clothes from her body and survey it with an insolence that drove the colour from her skin.

'And another man's child? Is this too of no importance?'

'You wouldn't,' Danielle breathed painfully.

His face grim, Jourdan assured her briefly, 'I would do anything to secure my position in this

country—my   country—*mignonne*.   Anything.
Now, do we understand one another?'

'My stepfather will never forgive you for this!'
Danielle stormed. 'I don't know how you've
managed to persuade the Sheikha to be a party to
this . . . this atrocity, but when my stepfather . . .'

'The Sheikha agreed because, like me, she has
the good of this country very close to her heart,
and as for your stepfather—my uncle,' he leaned
forward all of a sudden, forcing Danielle to bend
backwards to avoid contact with his body, 'am I
not giving him what he wanted all along?'

He smiled cruelly when he saw the acknowledgement flaring betrayingly in Danielle's eyes.

'You see, *mignonne*,' he said softly, 'you yourself
acknowledge the truth. My uncle may not be
pleased with the way in which our marriage is
accomplished, but the fact of its accomplishment
will please him mightily . . .'

'But I don't love you,' Danielle stormed
bitterly, 'and you don't love me All you want is to
gain control of the oil company.'

'This I acknowledge,' Jourdan agreed, his face
slowly hardening. 'You must have thought me a
fool indeed, daughter of Hassan, if you imagined
I would stand passively by while all I had worked
for was given elsewhere, to a boy such as Saud.'

'Saud!' Danielle stared fearfully up at him. Was
this the reason for her abduction and enforced
marriage? Because Jourdan thought she might
have fallen in love with Saud?

'Strange as it may seem to you,' she said coldly,
'I do not run after men who are betrothed to
others . . .'

'Saud, or some other, it makes little difference,'

Jourdan remarked with a cool shrug. 'You are ripe for marriage, Danielle, and I shall not have the fruit I have tended so long plucked by others, rather I will pluck it myself, even though it still be a little unripe and green.'

'I hate you!' Danielle burst out, unable to bear either his mockery or hard intent any longer. 'I suppose the only reason you've finally given your magnanimous approval to my parents' marriage is because you realised it was the only way you were going to get the oil company. Tell me something,' she demanded sarcastically. 'Has any decision in your life ever been governed by anything but self-interest?'

'Once,' Jourdan replied coolly. 'When I thought a person of whom I was very fond was making a bad mistake. We quarrelled bitterly about it, and I lost the man who had been father, uncle and friend to me all my young life.'

Danielle let out her breath on a faint hiss, knowing he was referring to her stepfather.

'But once you realised that the marriage was working, that the only way you could get control of the oil company was by accepting the marriage, your scruples disappeared? Very commendable,' Danielle sneered.

'You speak without knowledge, daughter of Hassan,' Jourdan said abruptly. 'I shall leave you to your maid. The marriage takes place within the hour.' He paused by the door. 'And be very sure it is legal and watertight. We shall be married according to the laws of Qu'Har and those of my church. There will be no annulment; no divorce.'

The words rang on in Danielle's ears, long after Jourdan had left her. Beyond the perimeter of the bed she could hear Zanaide moving about softly.

'I have prepared the Sitt's bath,' Zanaide said coaxingly. 'I have perfumed it with oils to ensure fertility and . . .'

'I don't want a bath, Zanaide,' Danielle told her abruptly. She wasn't going to allow herself to be perfumed and prepared for this marriage like a sacrifice for the altar!

Marriage! Her fists clenched in helplessly impotent rage. This couldn't be happening. Fate couldn't be condemning her to this travesty of a marriage—but it was.

The only thing that got her off the bed and into the billowing crimson and gold chiffon caftan was Jourdan's parting threat that he would come and dress her himself, and even then it was with distasteful reluctance, refusing to even glance at her reflection in the floor-to-ceiling mirrors which lined one wall of the room.

'The Sitt does not like the caftan?' Zanaide asked reproachfully. 'The Sheikha herself ordered its design and execution. The pearl buttons are her gift to you.'

The Sheikha who had deliberately gone behind her back and conspired with Jourdan, as though she were nothing more than a slave girl sold to the highest bidder, Danielle thought bitterly. And why? Because her stepfather was in control of Qu' Har's oil. Jourdan had married her for that sole purpose. Well, if she could not prevent the marriage, she could at least make sure that not a single day passed without her reiterating to Jourdan how much she hated it—and him!

'And now the girdle,' Zanaide murmured reverently, breaking into Danielle's thoughts, and

coming towards her carefully carrying a heavy,
intricately chased belt of silver studded with
emeralds and diamonds.

'This girdle belongs to the family of Sheikh
Jourdan,' Zanaide explained. 'It is the custom for
the women of the house to dress the bride and
fasten the girdle.' As she spoke she slid the heavy
weight round Danielle's slender waist, where it
lay like iron hands, imprisoning her, Danielle
thought, shivering under its ice-cold embrace, the
myriad flashing points of colour from the precious
stones hypnotising her into a strange state of lethargy where nothing seemed to matter any longer.
Too late she remembered the mint tea Zanaide
had coaxed her into drinking and the sense of relaxation which had followed almost immediately.

'Zanaide.' Was that whisper of sound really her
own voice?

'The Sitt wishes for something?'

'What was in that tea you gave me?' Danielle
demanded urgently, wishing she could escape
from the increasing sense of lethargy pervading
her body and clouding her mind.

'Nothing harmful. It was just a little of the
poppy drug,' Zanaide soothed. 'The Sheikh
ordered it so. It is quite common for girls to drink
thus before their marriage. It soothes the mind
and relaxes the body.'

Too concerned as she was with the coming
ceremony, it was to be some time before
Danielle realised the import of Zanaide's last
words. As the drug coaxed her stiffening muscles
into unwilling relaxation she allowed Zanaide to
to rub perfumed oils into her wrists and throat
and to add a touch of kohl beneath her eyes, im-

parting depth and lustre.

'You are ready,' Zanaide said at last, touching
the intricate fastenings of the silver girdle. 'Now
none but your husband may unfasten your girdle,
and then the pearls of chastity which conceal from
him the secret gardens of your body, where only
he may venture.'

Danielle wanted to cover her ears, so that she
wouldn't be forced to listen to what Zanaide was
saying, but even as she started to protest the door
opened and her heart started to pound with heavy
uneven strokes, her mouth dry as Zanaide led her
forward to the man waiting imperiously for her.

In his ceremonial robes Jourdan was an imposing, distant stranger, a man whose eyes rested
remotely on her trembling frame as white-clad
servants escorted them to a chamber overlooking
the now darkened courtyard which lay beyond
Danielle's own room.

The first service, in Arabic, was totally in-
comprehensible to Danielle, who made her responses in a voice as listless as an obedient child,
without truly comprehending their meaning.

For one brief moment as they stood before the
priest ten minutes later, Danielle contemplated
pleading with him to help her, but as though he
had read her mind, Jourdan's fingers bit cruelly
into her arm, his eyes totally pitiless as he
murmured dulcetly, 'I wouldn't if I were you,
daughter of Hassan. According to the Muslim law
you are already my wife, my possession, and I
shall be entitled to punish you as I think fit if you
anger me . . .'

With that threat ringing in her ears, Danielle
stumbled through her responses, the words stick-

ing in her aching throat as she acknowledged their import and finality.

'And now, *mon fils*, you may kiss the bride,' the old priest announced with a smile, closing his bible, and Danielle's body clenched in panicky rejection as she felt Jourdan turn towards her, his hands on her shoulders. She could feel his eyes upon her, but refused to look at him, holding her breath tensely, expecting with every passing second to feel the hateful possession of his mouth on hers.

When it didn't come she glanced upwards, surprised by the smile curling his mouth, until she realised that it didn't extend to his eyes, which remained as cold and alert as a falcon's sighting its prey.

'I think in view of my bride's very evident shyness that that is a pleasure I must reserve for later, Father,' Jourdan drawled easily. 'Mahmoud will show you to your room, and thank you once again for your good services.

'Father Pierre came out here before the Second World War and has remained ever since,' Jourdan explained when he had gone and they were alone. 'Through him my uncle made good his vow to my mother that I should be brought up in her religion.'

It was the first time he had told her anything without either mockery or anger, but Danielle stubbornly refused to respond.

'If you will just summon Zanaide to escort me back to my room,' she said coldly, 'I'm tired and I should like to go to bed.'

Something smouldered smokily in the dark eyes, instantly doused, and Jourdan's voice was completely expressionless as he said silkily.

'So should I, *mignonne*, but you have no need of Zanaide to escort you to your room. I shall do so myself ... I had not realised my new bride would be so anxious to consummate the vows we have just made. A little old-fashioned of me, perhaps,' he added cruelly, 'but I had thought I would be the one to suggest that we retire. I find your eagerness refreshing.'

He was openly smiling now, laughter lighting the dark depths of his eyes, but Danielle was white and rigid with shock, her eyes enormous in her small pale face.

'You can't mean it.' she stammered wildly, forgetting caution in her anxiety to be assured that she had misunderstood. 'You don't want me ... It was just to get the oil company ...'

'Which I have to keep,' Jourdan said coldly, his laughter banished. 'You are my wife, Danielle, and by the time dawn pearls the morning sky you will be in deed as well as word.'

'No!'

The word was ripped from Danielle's throat, panic flaring hotly through tensed limbs as she turned frantically towards the door, but once again Jourdan had anticipated her, his fingers tightening painfully around her wrist as she tried to pull away.

'You will behave from now on as befits my wife,' he gritted against her ear, 'and not as the foolish child you undoubtedly are. A room has been prepared for us. Come ...'

A tiny whimper of protest broke past Danielle's compressed lips as Jourdan's grip tightened, but she remained steadfastly glued to the floor, determination giving way to fear as he turned, and with one swift, lithe movement swung her up into his arms.

'Your bones are as fragile as those of the gazelle who graze by the oasis,' he murmured mockingly as he carried her out of the room and up a flight of narrow stairs into a chamber whose magnificence would, in other circumstances, have completely taken Danielle's breath away.

As it was, the rich draperies in crimson and gold embroidered brocades; the brilliant Persian rugs and the overall masculinity of the apartment, combined with the heady fragrances of sandalwood and incense, completely overwhelmed her.

She was placed on a low divan, amongst a nest of silken cushions, Jourdan's lithe frame between her and the imposing bed to which her eyes were unwillingly drawn.

'So very apprehensive,' Jourdan mocked, following her glance, 'Never mind, *mignonne*, before morning streaks the sky you will have learned to look upon the place where you entered the doorway of womanhood with different eyes.'

'Those of hatred,' Danielle confirmed bitterly. 'If you had the slightest scrap of compassion or civilisation you would never even dream of doing this . . .'

'You think not? How very naïve you are, *mignonne*,' Jourdan mocked softly. 'There cannot be many men who have looked upon you and not dreamed of enjoying exactly what I shall be enjoying tonight.'

The room whirled dizzily about her as Danielle tried to moan another anguished protest. She saw Jourdan coming towards her and flinched beneath

both his presence and the icy lash of his tongue as
he swore vehemently.

'Drink this.'

The command could not be ignored, but even
as she took the first mouthful of hot sweet mint
tea, warning bells flashed through Danielle's
mind. She tried to pull back, but the pressure of
Jourdan's fingers on her neck prevented her, just
as his steely determination prevented her from
refusing to drink the hot tea, which she was sure
was drugged, just as her earlier cup had been.
Now with hideous clarity she remembered
Zanaide telling her that it relaxed the mind and
the body. She shivered violently, her over-active
imagination conjuring up pictures of what she was
going to be called upon to endure, her will
weakened by the drug she had been given. She
longed to sob and plead to be set free, but pride
would not let her.

'So much fear and trepidation,' Jourdan
murmured softly, his fingers closing on her
throat. 'Will it help you, I wonder, daughter of
Hassan, if I tell you that not so many days from
now you will welcome with open arms that which
you now fear?'

'Impossible!' Danielle choked out fiercely.

The anguished thudding of her heart was
blotted out by Jourdan's spontaneous laughter, as
his hands slid from the warm flesh of her throat
to the cold girdle encircling her waist.

'All things are possible, Danielle,' he drawled
laconically. 'And if you are honest with yourself,
you will admit that this is so.'

Danielle's head dropped back against his
shoulder as he lifted her in his arms and carried

her over to the enormous bed. Her eyes squeezed
tightly closed, her body tensed against his touch,
Danielle lay there hardly daring to breathe. One
by one she heard Jourdan extinguish the lights
which had illuminated the room, and then he was
beside her on the bed, his hands making short
work of the intricate girdle, his breath against her
cheek as he reached for the first of the pearl buttons.

CHAPTER SEVEN

As Danielle froze beneath the questing fingers, she squeezed her eyes closed, unable to bear the sight of the lean brown fingers against the paleness of her flesh.

The night air lay like silk against her skin. Her heart seemed to be pounding with a heavy insistence outside all her previous experience. She felt the warmth of Jourdan's breath against her cheek and purposefully turned away, her lips tightening, only to part on a shocked gasp as she felt the cool brush of his mouth not against her own trembling lips but in the pale vee of flesh exposed by the unfastened buttons at the neck of her caftan.

As the deft fingers slid more pearls from their looped fastenings, Jourdan's mouth moved downwards, until it rested in the valley between her breasts, her heart racing beneath the male hand covering it.

As though the wild urgency of her thudding heart conveyed a secret to Jourdan she could not share, Danielle saw him raise his head and watch her through the darkness, his eyes glinting like a cat's and silvered by the moon.

'There is nothing to fear, daughter of Hassan,' he told her in a voice as soft and sweet as honey. 'Come, give me your hand and together we shall walk the paths of the Garden of Eden.'

Like someone in a trance Danielle found herself responding, even though it was against her will.

Her trembling fingers were taken and spread against the heated warmth of Jourdan's chest, beneath the robe he had worn for the marriage ceremony.

'Your fingers flutter like the wings of a trapped bird,' he said softly. 'I am only as other men, *mignonne*, my flesh much as theirs . . .'

But he wasn't like any other man she knew, Danielle thought wildly. They did not demand that she touch them so intimately, so that her fingers could not help respond to the vibrant male life beneath them. Nor did they hold her so close that her soft breasts were crushed against hard muscles and scraped by crisp, dark body hair, whose touch was doing strange things to her tensed stomach muscles, causing them to relax into a melting weakness which made it impossible for her to do anything but murmur a small protest as her caftan was removed completely, along with the dubious protection of Jourdan's arms as he turned her sideways so that the full moon silvered the slender length of her body, revealing how it trembled nervously beneath his lazy scrutiny.

Confused and disturbed by the hitherto unknown sensations awakening within her, Danielle moved, gasping faintly as she realised that Jourdan was as naked as she was herself, the same moon which had silvered her tender flesh highlighting the broad shoulders and tautly muscled male outline, her eyes lifting fearfully to those of the man watching her so impassively, mutely begging for a stay of sentence.

'It is too late, Danielle,' Jourdan muttered in a voice alien to his normal laconic tone. 'Even if my mind did not urge me to this course, my flesh does. You are beautiful beyond belief; as slender as the young gazelle who flees the hunter, and just as provocative. One lean finger touched her cheek, turning her towards him, where he surveyed the silver streaks of tears dispassionately. 'You weep like a child, frightened of the unknown, but already womanhood beckons you, although you will not admit it. I will not leave the fruit which is rightfully mine ripening on the tree for other hands to pluck.'

Danielle's anguished protest was lost beneath the mouth that plundered and then softened, coaxing her stubborn lips into parting in tremulous wonder.

No one had ever kissed her like this before, she acknowledged half deliriously as Jourdan's hands slid down her back, moulding her yielding body to the hard warmth of his, his lips continuing to tease and coax until her hands went pleadingly to his shoulders, surrender in the huge, bemused eyes she lifted in shaken supplication to his.

It must be the drug she had been given, she decided muzzily, there could be no other reason for this strange, melting need to yield herself completely to the heady persuasion of Jourdan's lips and hands. Her mouth parted automatically, her head falling back over his supporting arm, her senses reeling as he probed and explored the sweet softness she had previously withheld from him, and as though he knew that the kiss conceded defeat his hand stroked firmly over her breast, arousing sensations that made Danielle reel in fresh astonishment. Somewhere deep down inside her a small voice warned her that later she would regret this heady intoxication which told her to respond blindly to the sensations Jourdan was arousing, but his hold on her was so strong that even had she heeded it it would have been impossible for her to break away from him.

Her hands moved instinctively from his shoulders over the hard muscles of his back and downward, drawing a muttered protest from the lips exploring the pulsing softness of her throat, and were redirected along paths she had never in her wildest dreams imagined—or wanted to imagine—taking.

Beneath her shy exploration she could feel the satin texture of Jourdan's skin, damply warm where she touched it, filling her with a primeval feeling of power she could barely understand, but which made it imperative for her to press her body deeper into the hard masculinity of his, running her fingers over the long back and taut muscles, until her touch drew a husky protest and Jourdan's lips left the slender curve of her throat to tease the full softness of her breasts, already burgeoning to soft roundness beneath his skilled fingers.

Driven farther and farther from reality along paths of sensuality which held her fast within their grip, Danielle had no conscious knowledge of arching instinctively beneath Jourdan's hard hands, or of the way they trembled slightly as his tongue touched her nipple, circling it slowly, sending her mindless with a pleasure which overwhelmed modesty and caution and left only a need for something which ached deep down inside her and grew stronger with every passing second.

'You learn well, Danielle,' she heard Jourdan mutter hoarsely before his mouth closed in implicit demand on the tautly tempting outline of her breast. He added something in Arabic which sounded like a plea, but Danielle's mind was too fuzzy to comprehend it. She was caught in the middle of a raging tide, too confused and bemused to try and fight it, and when Jourdan's hands slid down to her hips, lifting her slightly and coaxing her slim thighs apart with the burning heat of his own she could only look at him through the darkness and feel the cramping excitement race through her body at the intimate contact with his.

By the time the mists of sexual pleasure had parted enough for her to appreciate what the pulsing hardness of his body betokened it was too late.

Her sharp cry of pain and distress was lost beneath the firm pressure of Jourdan's lips, but fear swamped her earlier exultation, pleasure giving way to shocked acknowledgement of what had happened. The drugs she had been given had caused this, Danielle thought shakily, brushing away the tears she was trying to subdue. She hated Jourdan as she had never hated anyone in her life before. She tried to move away, but he wouldn't let her, his face a white mask of fury above her, and she realised that she had voiced her thoughts out loud.

'You don't hate me, *mignonne*,' he drawled with harsh cruelty, his fingers biting into the tender flesh of her arms. 'You hate yourself for being a woman . . .'

'You drugged me!' Danielle stormed back at him, falling back against the pillows as the hands which had been tender suddenly tightened and with calculated cruelty held her prisoner while his body reinforced its domination of her own.

'Stop it!' Danielle protested furiously. 'Aren't

you satisfied with the degradation you've already inflicted on me?'

Fury mingled with a self-disgust she could barely admit surged through her until she feared nothing; not even the blazing anger burning in the darkness of Jourdan's eyes.

His possession of her was brutally swift, making her gasp in sudden pain, her fingers curling protestingly into his shoulders as his mouth punished hers, forcing her lips to part beneath his ruthless assault.

Quite when pain turned to heated pleasure Danielle did not know. One moment she was furious and bitterly resenting the intrusion of Jourdan's body, the next, or so it seemed later in her hazy recollections, she was responding to a sensation as primitive and age-old as man himself.

Her fingers were still curled into the hard warmth of Jourdan's shoulders, but now with pleasure instead of pain, pleasure which beat at her in ever-increasing waves until she was moaning softly and involuntarily beneath the burning demand of Jourdan's mouth, her arms locking round his neck as her body arched with instinctive need to prolong the pleasure he was giving her, her heart racing frantically against his flesh as his harsh breathing communicated a message which seemed to be received in every part of her body.

The exquisite fulfilment of their lovemaking stayed locked inside Danielle's mind, even when her body had relaxed into exhausted satisfaction; Jourdan's tongue delicately tasting the tears lying damply on her cheeks her last memory as sleep claimed her.

CHAPTER EIGHT

IT was daylight. In her drowsy, half awakened state Danielle could feel the warmth of the sun's rays through the draperies of the bed. She stretched, unconscious seduction in the languorous movement, her body full of a strange lethargy which made it impossible for her to jump out of bed with her normal vigour. She rolled sideways, her eyes clouding as fragments of a nightmare came back to her, her body tensing with horror as she remembered events which had been no nightmare, but cold, factual reality.

The bathroom door opened and Jourdan strode into the room, a towel draped casually over his lean-hipped frame, its white softness in direct contrast to his tanned body. A bitter hatred filled Danielle as he walked casually over to the bed and looked down at her. Her first instinct was to turn away from the amused comprehension of his glance, but she forced herself to meet it with eyes carefully blanked of all emotion.

'Well, *ma chérie*, did I not keep my promise?' Jourdan drawled, one lean hand pushing aside the bedcovers to trace the fragile bones of her shoulder.

'Your promise? I call it a threat!' Danielle spat furiously at him, pulling away from his hand. 'I suppose I've one thing to be grateful for—at least now that our marriage can't be annulled I won't have to bear your loathesome touch on my body again!'

'Loathesome?' Danielle was too caught up in her own emotions to hear the warning tone in the softly spoken word. 'You didn't seem to find it loathesome at the time, *mignonne*, far from it,' Jourdan reminded her hatefully, 'In fact unless my memory serves me wrong you pleaded with me to open the gates of paradise for you . . .'

'Because you drugged me,' Danielle cried wildly. 'Otherwise I would never . . .'

'Drugged you?' The forbidding words cut across her bitter protests. 'Your imagination runs away with you, daughter of Hassan. The only drug that was used, if you can call it that, was your female response to my maleness.'

'That tea you made me drink was drugged, just like the cup Zanaide gave me,' Danielle protested furiously. 'Otherwise I would never have . . . have . . .'

'Responded to me with such sweet passion?' Jourdan suggested cruelly. 'I did not use drugs, Danielle, it wasn't necessary,' he told her sardonically. 'However, if you should prefer me to prove my point . . .?'

He was reaching for the towel even as he spoke, and to her chagrin Danielle felt herself crimson furiously, her body going rigid as her eyes mutely begged for the compassion her lips refused to ask for.

'Still such a child,' Jourdan said acidly, leaning over her, his hands either side of her body, imprisoning her in the bed. 'It might be amusing to teach you a lesson you well deserve, *petite*. It would take very little to arouse those passionate fires you keep so well hidden, to the point where every night not spent in my arms would be the most exquisite torture . . .'

'You . . . you . . . sadist!' Danielle hissed at him, driven almost beyond words in her need to show him the depths of her hatred and contempt for him. It was on the tip of her tongue to tell him that there was no way she was going to remain his wife with that threat hanging over her, but caution intervened, reminding her that for now she was virtually a prisoner within his castle, and that no Arab would lift a hand to help a runaway wife. There must be some way she could escape, she reasoned. If she could just telephone her parents. One phone call that would be enough to have them both on a plane to Qu'Har.

'When you have finished sulking you may summon Zanaide to help you dress. I am going out riding. If you behave yourself I may take you with me another day, when we have been married a little longer. Were I to allow you to ride this morning my men would think me a poor bride-groom, so today you must occupy yourself alone.'

Try as she might Danielle could not control her shocked gasp, or the vivid colour burning her heated skin. Her hands curled impotently until her nails were digging in her palms, the tears stinging her eyes preventing her from seeing Jourdan leave the room.

Once he had gone she did not give way to her emotions, telling herself that she would not give him the pleasure of having it whispered amongst his household that he had made her cry, and so when Zanaide came in carrying her breakfast tray she found Danielle sitting up in bed, manicuring her nails.

Food would surely choke her, Danielle thought sickly, barely glancing at the fresh warm rolls and honey Zanaide had brought her and the sweet, juicy dates, but the young maid protested when Danielle said that she didn't want anything, her expression demurely coy as she murmured that Danielle must keep up her strength.

'The Sheikha will not make a fine son if she does not eat,' Zanaide told her.

A son! Danielle's stomach clenched protestingly, her face paling as the full implication of Zanaide's innocent words struck her. Dear God, please not that, she prayed with chattering teeth as she made a pretence of eating one of the rolls. She had to leave Qu'Har, and at once. She couldn't endure to spend another day here, especially not in this room, haunted by the memory of her own aroused breathing and soft, panting cries.

Zanaide helped her to bathe and dress in one of the caftans the Sheikha had ordered for her, and although the younger girl's eyes widened fractionally as she saw the faint purpling bruises on Danielle's fair skin, where Jourdan's passion had made her forget pain, she said nothing.

After breakfast and with Zanaide as interpreter Danielle was shown over the castle by a tall bearded Arab who Zanaide told her was Jourdan's comptroller.

The castle was enormous; one entire wing, although furnished, appeared unused, but Zanaide told her that it was set aside for the use of the desert nomads who were allowed to water their herds at the castle's oasis twice a year and for that time remained under the castle roof.

'The Sheikh has done much for our people,' Zanaide told Danielle seriously as they explored a beautiful inner courtyard, which the comptroller had told Danielle was to be her own special province. 'Our young men learn of the new technology at foreign universities, our girls are permitted to go to school.'

Permitted! Danielle's lip curled faintly. She and Zanaide were worlds apart in their outlook. What Zanaide looked upon as a privilege given by an indulgent male Danielle considered to be hers without question. She shivered suddenly despite the heat, as she dwelt on what her future life could be if she didn't escape from Qu'Har. He owned her, Jourdan had told her calmly last night, and her heart still burned with the resentment his arrogant words had aroused.

Zanaide drew her attention to the beauty of the mosaic-tiled floor of the courtyard, but Danielle merely gave it a desultory glance. A cage was a cage no matter how prettily it was painted. An unbearable longing to be free of the castle and all that it represented overwhelmed her. Shielding her eyes from the fierce glare of the sun, she looked around her. A tower, soaring above the tiled roofs of the castle, caught her eye and she stared up at it.

'That is the Sheikh's private place,' Zanaide told her eagerly, patently relieved that something had caught Danielle's attention. 'It was built by an ancestor of the Sheikh's who used it to watch the heavens and make predictions from what he read there.'

'Can we go up and see it?' Danielle asked slowly, something deep down inside her reaching out towards the tower. Zanaide looked upset and shocked.

'It is the private apartment of the Sheikh,' she told Danielle apologetically, 'and none may go there but him.' She smiled suddenly. 'But now that you are married perhaps he will invite you to share its solitude with him. He spends many hours there . . .'

Doing what? Danielle wondered acidly, trying not to admit to the feeling of disappointment growing inside her as she realised that the tower—like her freedom—was withheld from her, and by the same man.

Danielle had been at the castle in the desert for nearly a week. Jourdan had not been near her since their wedding night. She had spent the second night of their marriage lying in the vast bed in a state of rigid hatred, admitting only with the first pearly fingers of dawn that her efforts had all been in vain and that Jourdan was not going to give her the opportunity to prove his arrogant claims wrong and repulse him with the icy disdain with which she had intended to greet him. She was asleep when the bedroom door opened and the morning sun threw the tall shadow of a man across her bed, a frown in his eyes as he surveyed the tumbled disorder of her hair and the mauve shadows beneath her eyes.

It was Zanaide who told her of the small child who had been lost by one of the tribes who still wandered the desert, and how Jourdan and his men had spent the night searching for the little boy.

'The little one was fortunate that the Sheikh was here to organise the search,' Zanaide had told her. 'Otherwise he would probably never have been found. Just as the heat of our sun during the day can kill, so can the chill of it by night.'

There had been celebrations at the nomad camp by the oasis following the safe return of the little boy, or so Zanaide had informed Danielle. The servants seemed to know everything, and Danielle's cheeks burned to think that they must also know how unwillingly she had been made the bride of the man whose word they took as law, and how ruthlessly he had overridden that unwillingness. Her one hope was that her parents would telephone her from America, and on being unable to get in touch with her would realise that something was wrong and come straight out to Qu'Har. Danielle didn't for one moment doubt that her stepfather would leave no stone unturned to have her marriage set aside once he knew how it had been accomplished and how much she hated it, firmly ignoring the small voice which told her tauntingly that there had been a good deal of truth in what Jourdan had said about her stepfather accepting the marriage.

The days seemed to grow hotter, the sun burning brassily down from a sky whose blueness seemed to hurt the eyes. Zanaide urged Danielle to try to rest during the hottest part of the day, but Danielle could not. A restless urgency seemed to possess her, her nerves constantly tightening under the constant threat of coming face to face with her unwanted husband. Her normal composure deserting her under the pressure of the tension enveloping her Danielle found it almost impossible to eat, and Zanaide frowned over the amount of weight she was losing.

One afternoon when the heat of the courtyard seemed to push down on her in oppressive waves Danielle found herself moving with the slow purposefulness of a sleepwalker towards the stairs which led to Jourdan's tower.

She knew that he spent most evenings there alone—Zanaide had told her as much, flushing guiltily as though she were giving away some carefully guarded secret. What did the other girl think she would do? Danielle asked herself wearily. Surely she must realise that she had no more desire for Jourdan's company than he had for hers. Marriage to her and the consummation of that marriage had accomplished his purpose and now he had no further need of her.

The stone steps curved upwards spiral fashion and Danielle followed them blindly, not pausing to glance through the narrow slits let into the thick stone walls at intervals. It was cool on the stairs, shielded from the brilliance of the sun by the thick stone which Zanaide had told her had been quarried during the days of the Crusades and used to build this vast complex by the sophisticated and learned Muslim who had travelled widely with the victorious armies of Saladin.

The stairs came to an abrupt end before a barred and studded wooden door similar to those guarding the main entrance to the castle. Danielle stared at them, focusing properly for the first time. What on earth was she doing up here? She looked back behind her, trying to remember what impulse had driven her to climb the stairs in the first place. She had been sitting in the courtyard, watching the carp in the fishpond, their freedom as curtailed as hers, when suddenly a yearning to see as far beyond her prison walls as she could had overcome her.

The door to the tower yielded beneath her touch and Danielle stepped inside, the door closing behind her unnoticed as her eyes widened.

Silky Persian rugs adorned the floor, shimmering silk gauzes veiled the walls shimmering iridescent with all the colours of a peacock's tail—no soft pastel shades here but luxury and richness of an opulence that caught Danielle's breath. The tower was circular with divans set in the window embrasures, covered in furs. A telescope—a curiously mundane article in such an exotic setting—caught Danielle's eye, and she wandered over to it, touching the smooth wood absently, her eyes drawn to the distant horizon. If only she could find some way of leaving Qu'Har! A tear slid down her cheek, quickly followed by another, and she brushed them away impatiently. How Jourdan would love to see her like this, defeated and in tears! Her fingers clenched, her chin lifting proudly. As she turned towards the door she saw the narrow bed she had not noticed before, was this where Jourdan slept? With an effort of will she dragged her eyes away, hating herself for the inner tremor which wracked at her, reminding her of all the things she had fought so hard to forget—like the rich satin feel of Jourdan's skin beneath her shy fingertips. The overwhelming sense of weakness she had experienced before his superior strength, the trembling, burgeoning arousal of her own body, quickening through curiosity to mindless desire as he set it on fire with his hands and lips, and she . . .

'No!'

The word was torn from her throat on an an-

guished cry. She had responded only because of
the tea she had drunk—tea she knew had been
drugged despite his denials. There could be no
other possible explanation for the wild abandon
of her final capitulation to his arrogant dominance. Could there?

All at once a terrible weariness overcame her,
an aching pain in the region of her heart and
throat, a burning sensation behind her heavy
eyelids presaging tears. What was happening to
her? Danielle wondered wretchedly. Where was
her determination, her independence? She lay
down on the narrow bed and closed her eyes
merely intending to rest them for a moment.

The sound of someone moving intruded on
Danielle's dream. It had been such a happy one
too. She had been back in London. Back with her
parents. She sighed, her hand reaching up toward
her stiff neck, her voice strained as she called
Zanaide's name.

'The maid, unlike the mistress, does not dare
to penetrate the eagle's lair,' a cool male voice
drawled softly. 'What are you doing here, *petite*?
Or am I to draw my own conclusions from your
presence here in this tower which is my preserve
and mine alone?'

He had come to stand beside her. Danielle was
conscious of him with every nerve ending, despite
the darkness of the room, which had, with the
coming of night grown cold. How could she have
managed to fall asleep up here?

'Draw whatever conclusions you wish,' she told
Jourdan bitterly. 'But the truth is . . .' She
paused, her eyes focusing blindly on the stars
shining so brightly outside the narrow windows.

'The truth is that I came up here because I wanted to be free. I wanted to see the world beyond the confines of your kingdom . . .'

Jourdan's harshly indrawn breath warned her that she had gone too far, her gasp of pain ignored as his fingers bit deeply into her arms and he hauled her to her feet and dragged her over to the window.

'Look as far as you like, *mignonne*,' he whispered harshly. 'But while your eyes are fixed on the earth, the horizon, however distant it may be, still belongs to me.'

Danielle shuddered as she felt his breath on the back of her neck, his mirthless laughter as cold as the night air.

'Come . . .'

His fingers on her arm propelled her back into the room and directed her to where the telescope was fixed on its stand.

'The man who built this castle was crushed beneath a block of stone when it was being erected. Although his life was spared he was left a cripple, and it was then that he had this observatory built.'

Danielle was standing before the telescope. She shivered briefly as Jourdan's arms closed round her, but his touch was completely impersonal, his hands directing her to look through the glass to the stars beyond.

'Freedom is a state of mind, *mignonne*,' he said against her hair. 'My ancestor found it in this room, studying the constellations, even though physically he was a prisoner of his own infirmity. Other men are prisoners of their own emotions, their hearts given in bondage to a woman as cold and remote as the distant stars.'

'And I am your prisoner,' Danielle finished bitterly.

'No, *ma chérie*.' The telescope was removed and she was forced to meet the sardonic mockery in Jourdan's eyes. 'You are a prisoner of your own pride, for without that you would surely admit that marriage to me has its . . . compensations . . .'

He could have meant many things; after all, he was an extremely wealthy and powerful man and no doubt many women would find those irresistible lures, but Danielle knew instinctively that he was referring to her body's treacherous betrayal of her, and her face flamed with the knowledge.

She walked unsteadily towards the door.

'Where are you going?'

The silky words halted her. She turned, probing the darkness to find the tall white-robed figure, his face masked by the shadows.

Somehow, without her being aware of him moving, he had interposed the bulk of his body between herself and the door. She stared at him, hoping he wouldn't see the fear leaping suddenly to life in her eyes.

'I want to go to my room.'

It was both an answer to his question and a demand, and Danielle realised that she had made a tactical error the moment the words were uttered. Something—and she feared it could only be anger—leaped to life in the dark eyes which lingered with insolent intensity on the firm thrust of her breasts beneath the flimsy chiffon robe Zanaide had chosen from her wardrobe.

'Your room?'

There was a world of meaning in the two softly

drawled words and Danielle found to her chagrin that her pulse rate had suddenly quickened, her breath coming in short nervous gasps. Jourdan was deliberately trying to unnerve her, she told herself, that was all; he could have as little desire to repeat the events of their wedding night as she; he was a man of the world, used to women as skilled at lovemaking as he was himself, and she . . .

Her cheeks burned as she remembered how completely she had abandoned herself to the delights of Jourdan's touch in those few final minutes when everything else had ceased to exist.

'Stop playing with me, Jourdan!' she stormed, trying to banish the insidious memory of his hands on her skin. 'You want me as little as I want you . . .'

'I wouldn't be so sure—on either count,' Jourdan murmured with a soft mockery that sent the fine hairs at the back of Danielle's neck standing up on end in alarm.

All at once he was far too close for comfort—close enough for her to breathe in the wholly male scent of his body mingling with the spicy tang of cologne. She tried to step back, but the white flash of his teeth as his lips parted in a smile warned her that he had seen through her artless movement and knew quite well why she wanted to avoid him.

This suspicion was borne out when his arm lifted and hard fingers grasped her chin.

'Why the virginal fear, *mignonne*?' he asked softly. 'You are my wife in fact as well as law, and in the cool of the nights when the sands of the desert shift restlessly beneath the stars is it not only natural that a man should seek solace in the arms of a woman. Are you woman enough for me to find solace in your arms, Danielle?' he asked, the timbre of his voice deepening huskily and causing Danielle to tremble with emotions his presence and touch suddenly brought to life. Caught fast in the grip of some strange paralysis, she was powerless to move, even when Jourdan's head lowered.

Her heart seemed to stand still. The room was virtually in darkness. Jourdan still grasped her chin, but the quality of his touch changed from that of a goaler to a lover.

His lips felt cool and firm. Danielle's trembled beneath them, her instincts urging her to flee.

'You are my wife,' Jourdan reminded her huskily against her lips. 'My companion of the night . . . Shall we share together once more the pleasure we enjoyed on our wedding night? Is that why I found you in my own private domain? Were you waiting for me, Danielle?'

She wanted to deny it, but the words were never allowed to be uttered. Jourdan's lips were trailing fire against her throat and lower, pushing aside the frail chiffon and finding unerringly the taut peaks of her breasts. His shoulder bones were hard beneath her fingers and she clung mindlessly to them, making no demur when her robe was pushed aside to reveal the slender beauty of her body.

'Jourdan?'

Her uncertain murmur was crushed beneath the hard warmth of the male mouth imposing its dominance against the softness of her flesh, her inarticulate cry lost as Jourdan lifted her in his arms and carried her across to the low divan.

This time Danielle could not blame any drug for the uninhibited passion of her own response; unless it was the mind-bending force of Jourdan's kisses, the knowledgeable touch of his hands on her skin, teaching her pleasure and making her shudder deeply with the intensity of her response.

'Is this what you came up here for, Danielle?'

The cold words froze the passionate warmth of her response. What on earth was she doing? She could hardly blame Jourdan for looking at her with such open contempt. She tore herself free of his grasp and ran towards the door, careless of the curt command he ground out behind her.

The cold night air of the stairs felt like ice against her exposed skin, and she was trembling when she reached her own room. For once Zanaide was not there waiting for her. Thankfully Danielle tore off her robe and ran a bath, plunging into the warm water and soaping herself vigorously. What had come over her? For a moment in Jourdan's arms she had experienced . . . Her busy hands stilled and the scented water started to cool. Why had she run away from Jourdan? Because she was frightened of him? Or because she was frightened of herself and the emotions he aroused within her?

Very slowly she climbed out of the bath and started to dry herself, her eyes enormous in her pale face.

For a moment in Jourdan's arms she had forgotten that he was her enemy; had forgotten what he had done to her; how he had cheated her and known only that he was the man who had brought her body to life, who had released a fountain of emotion deep down inside her such as she had never dreamed she possessed.

With a small, almost inarticulate cry, Danielle flung herself on her bed, her body shaking with soundless sobs as she forced herself to face the truth. She had gone up to the turret room not because she wanted to see the far distant horizon but because she had wanted to be close to the man whose room it was; the man whom she had married in hatred and whom she now . . . loved.

How could she? Logically it was impossible. Since when had the emotions been guided by logic? Danielle asked herself cynically. Her response to Jourdan's touch this evening had not been that of a woman who hated or was indifferent . . . She stared sightlessly into the darkness. Now, more than ever, it was imperative that she leave Qu'Har. A deep shudder wracked her as she dwelt on Jourdan's likely reaction to the discovery that she had fallen in love with him. How he would mock her! The long mouth would curl in cynical disdain. He would reach for her and . . .

Shivering, Danielle curled into a small tight ball, her flesh on fire with the memory of Jourdan's hands against it. She had to find a way of leaving the castle before she made a complete fool of herself and was forced to admit to Jourdan her longing for him. Even now, knowing what she knew, there was still regret that she had not stayed in the turret room. If she had done so, she would not now be sleeping alone in this vast bed . . .

CHAPTER NINE

'THE Sheikha must not go too near the horses,' Zanaide warned Danielle protestingly. 'They belong to the Sheikh and can be dangerous to those they do not know.'

Danielle ignored her maid's comments, moving from stable to stable, her breath caught in wondering awe at the beauty of the pure-bred Arab mares. Several grooms were busily at work in the stable yard, and Danielle was conscious of being scrutinised discreetly as she walked amongst them. It was only by dint of pestering the comptroller that she had been allowed to visit the stables at all, and even then she doubted that she would have been allowed to do so if Jourdan hadn't been away.

A pain like a sharp knife twisted her heart. Where he was she didn't know. He had disappeared the morning after her visit to the turret room, and at first in his absence she had seen the means of her own escape. The comptroller had been polite, but firm, and all her efforts to beg or borrow a car had been met with a series of excuses. Jourdan must have give instructions that she was not to be allowed to leave the castle, Danielle thought bitterly, but somehow she must find a way of doing so, and soon—before Jourdan returned. His absence had been all she needed to convince her on that head, and she knew she could not trust herself not to betray her love for him when he did return.

The castle was a different place without him, and she ached for the sight of his tall robed figure, the sound of his voice, even his sardonic smile. She had never dreamed it was possible to feel like this about another human being, and the intensity of her emotions frightened her. Jourdan didn't want her as herself; all he wanted was the power marriage to her would give him, and even then not merely for his own benefit. How long would it be before he started to resent a marriage that was no marriage at all; a wife chosen simply because she was his uncle's stepdaughter? What was it Philippe had said about him? That there was a constant stream of beautiful women ready to throw themselves at his feet? Danielle could well believe it.

A servant came over and muttered something to the comptroller, who excused himself, returning to Danielle's side seconds later to explain that he was called away on business.

Left to her own devices, Danielle watched a couple of grooms preparing feed for the mares, an idea suddenly beginning to take shape in her mind.

'Tell one of the men to saddle a mount for me,' she instructed Zanaide. 'I want to ride out to the oasis.'

The oasis itself was several miles away from the castle, and althought Zanaide looked a little concerned she made no demur, speaking to one of the young grooms in rapid Arabic.

Seconds later he was leading a daintily prancing mare out into the cobbled yard for Danielle's inspection, his eyes resting appreciatively on her pale skin and flame-coloured hair.

'Tell him she will do very well,' Danielle told Zanaide, 'and that I will return in ten minutes.'

It took her less than that to change into her jeans and a thin but long-sleeved shirt. She had no idea how far she might have to ride—but certainly it would be farther than the oasis. She had no idea how far it was from the castle to the city, but surely it could not be too far; after all, Jourdan would scarcely live somewhere inaccessible to his business.

She could remember that they had travelled east out of the city, so if she headed west to begin with . . . Her mind working overtime, Danielle hurried back to the courtyard, where the young groom was still patiently holding the mare.

'I will ride with the Sheikha,' he began importantly, but Danielle shook her head.

· 'No, I wish to ride alone.' She was mounted before he could add any further protests, thankful for the riding lessons she had had all those years ago when she had been a pony-mad pre-adolescent. But excellent though they had been they had not really prepared her for a mount like her present one. 'Fleet as the wind' was how she had heard the Arab horses described, and now she knew what that meant. The little mare had a mouth as soft as velvet and seemed to need no instruction from Danielle to head for the oasis. However, she was well behaved enough to respond to Danielle's light touch on the reins, and thankfully Danielle curbed her eagerness to gallop along the sandy road. It would benefit neither of them if the little mare were allowed to tire herself out. Just for a moment she allowed herself to contemplate

Jourdan's reaction to her disappearance, but then she reminded herself that by the time he did she would be safely out of the country. She was going to demand that the Sheikha permitted her to return home. Urging the mare forward, Danielle ignored the small treacherous voice that whispered that she was a fool and that perhaps, with time, Jourdan might come to care for her. Why should he? For all his French blood he was a man of the East, brought up to hold women in contempt . . . Marriage to such a man could only in the long run destroy her.

The oasis was deserted. Danielle had expected to find at least a few wandering tribesmen resting beneath the shade of the palms, and she scanned the road uncertainly, checking that she was taking the correct fork.

The mare suddenly became obstinate, refusing to move. Danielle clicked her tongue, gently urging her forward, but the mare dug her heels in, her dainty ears twitching.

'What do you want?' Danielle demanded crossly when several minutes had passed. She was not going to be beaten by a mere animal!

At last she managed to get the mare to move. She had wasted valuable time at the oasis and as they trudged down the sandy track it seemed to her that the sun moved through the sky all too quickly. Soon it would be nightfall and she would be completely alone in the vastness of the desert with nothing before her but its emptiness. A feeling of panic seized her by the throat, and as though sensing it the mare sidled slightly, pawing at the ground.

Darkness fell swiftly, the sudden dropping of a

midnight velvet coat sprinkled with silver stars. Danielle had to rub her arms to ward off the cold, wishing she had thought to bring some means of protection, but she had expected to be in sight of some village if not the city itself long before now. She glanced at her watch, appalled to realise that she had been in the saddle for well over four hours. No wonder her back and thighs ached!

Darkness masked the landscape; relief at her escape began to give way to a fear which crept over her as inexorably as the fierce cold of the desert night. Even the little mare seemed less sure of herself. The high hopes with which Danielle had set out faded faster than the daylight. Her escape had been ill-planned and the result of a momentary impulse, she acknowledged, and now she was alone in the desert with no way of knowing where she was or where she was going. Too late memories of tales her stepfather had told her of the fate of unwary travellers in this harshly inhospitable land began to filter through her mind, her fingers tightening on the reins as fear mingled with tension. A cold wind sprang up out of nowhere, making her shiver, the little mare pricked up her ears as though in sympathy and Danielle felt tears blur her vision. She had been stupid and acted without forethought, and because of that both she and the mare could die here in this vast wilderness where only the eagle could survive unscathed.

The mare stumbled, almost throwing Danielle from the saddle, the reins slipped through her numb fingers and she reached desperately for them, praying that she wouldn't lose her seat. At least the mare was some companionship. In her

heart of hearts Danielle knew that there was only
one person with whom she would want to share
her present plight; one man who could banish her
fears with his presence and the cold with the
warmth of his body. A shuddering sigh trembled
through her. How quixotic it was that the very
man whose presence could banish her fears and
misery was the self-same one who had caused her
to flee from him into the desert in the first place—
her husband.

The little mare's ears pricked up and she
stopped for a moment. No matter how much
Danielle strained to part the darkness and see
what had halted her she could see nothing.
Thoughts of snakes and scorpions lurking unseen
on the ground below touched her spine with icy
fingers, and then just when she thought she would
have to dismount and lead the mare, Danielle felt
her move, uncertainly at first and then more
briskly as though guided by a voice beyond
human hearing. After a few seconds Danielle gave
up the battle of fighting against the mare and let
her have her head. She had no idea where they
were going; had in fact no idea where they were
or in which direction they had travelled. Above
them the moon shone coldly, a thin sickle moon,
silvering the landscape and turning the sands to
an endless rippling ocean.

Tired and exhausted, Danielle could barely stay
in the saddle. Her watch had stopped, but she
was sure they must have been travelling for hours.
For the first time she let her guard slip and
allowed her thoughts to drift to the castle and
everyone's reaction to her disappearance. They
would question the groom, of course, but all he

would be able to tell them was that she had intended to ride to the oasis. Too late Danielle remembered the search party which had been mounted to look for the small boy who had gone missing, but of course, Jourdan was not at the castle to organise one for her. Would the comptroller have sent him a message? Danielle shivered as she tried to picture his reaction to it. Would he care? Why should he? honesty compelled her to ask herself. Theirs was a marriage based on nothing but necessity. Were she to die her stepfather would scarcely blame Jourdan; after all, he had not been anywhere near the castle when she left.

Another new and even colder fear took possession of Danielle's heart; wild fancies driving out common sense and causing her to shiver with the deep conviction that far from sending out a search party, her husband was far more likely simply to leave her to her fate.

A combination of numbed limbs and nervous exhaustion aided by the rocking motion of the mare's walk lulled Danielle into the borderland between sleeping and waking. Her eyes closed, and although she was still conscious she seemed to have entered a dream world where everything around her took on a hazy, distant quality which combined with the numbing of her body to alleviate a little of her mental and physical agony.

When the oasis loomed up in front of her her eyelids had dropped over her eyes, her slender body slumped forward over the mare's neck. The little animal hesitated, snorting delicately and arching her neck as though trying to draw her rider's attention to their surroundings. Getting no response, she moved forward at a sedate walk, delicately picking her way across the sand.

How her subconscious managed to relay to her the presence of another shadow amongst so much darkness Danielle was not really sure. One moment her eyes were tightly closed, the next they flew open, her senses screaming a warning. The mare's reins were trailing in the sand, but by some miracle she had managed to avoid tripping in them. As she leaned forward to pat the mare's silky coat, Danielle's eyes searched the oasis for some indication of the presence which had awoken her. She could see nothing, but she knew she and the mare were not alone. The little horse was prancing skittishly on the sand, her body tensed as though awaiting a command. Fear drying her mouth, Danielle dismounted, her dismayed gasp suppressed as recognition of her surroundings finally came to her. They were at the oasis just beyond the castle. If she hadn't been so relieved to know where they were and so alarmed by the alien presence she sensed stalking her from the shadows, she might just have cried—cried for her own foolishness and both her own and the mare's exhaustion, but from somewhere she found the strength to stiffen her spine, and call out sharply, 'Who's there?'

The figure who stepped from the shadows was wearing riding clothes, his heavy dark cloak billowing in the cold breeze. The mare went immediately to him.

Apprehension shivered along Danielle's nerves, and she gasped as she saw and recognised his features. No wonder the horse had gone to him so eagerly! The mare was snorting happily with pleasure, her ears alert, as she nosed the man who was stroking her, plainly searching for some little treat.

'Jourdan, I thought you were away. How . . .'

The moment the words left her lips Danielle realised how foolish and damning they were. Plainly Jourdan thought so too. She could see the tight, angry line of his lips, the cold jet glitter of his eyes as they rested initially on her pale face, smudged with exhaustion and tears, and then on the mare.

'How did I find you?' His face was cold with reproof. 'I trusted Zara to have the sense you so obviously lack. The scent of water led her back here. It is an instinct without which animals die quickly and painfully in the desert,' he added curtly. 'Is this how our life together is going to be, *mignonne*? Every time I turn my back are you going to attempt to escape me?'

'I am not your possession,' Danielle objected tiredly. 'You lied and cheated, forced me into a marriage I didn't want. Can you blame me for wanting to escape?'

'From what and to what?' Jourdan asked softly. 'Can you tell me honestly that there have been no moments in our marriage which have brought you pleasure beyond anything you have known before?'

Danielle's expression betrayed her. Her face flamed in the darkness. Jourdan knew all her vulnerable points and how to make use of them. It was pointless telling her that she hated him, pointless railing against the fate which had brought them together, and for the first time she longed for an Arab girl's serene acceptance; her ability to smile and say softly, 'It is the will of Allah.'

'Come, you are falling asleep on your feet,' Jourdan said abruptly, taking her arm in one hand and the mare's reins in the other.

Danielle expected to be led to a Land Rover or car where others would be waiting, but to her surprise Jourdan led her instead to a clump of palm trees where his own mount was waiting. The mare whickered joyfully, and Jourdan smiled for the first time.

'Zara is not like you, *ma petite*,' he said mockingly. 'See how gladly she greets her mate. Have you no words of gratitude for me, Danielle, for rescuing you from the desert?'

'I wasn't lost,' Danielle retorted bitterly. 'You said so yourself. I suppose you've derived considerable amusement from imagining my fears, knowing all the time that Zara would bring me back to the oasis.'

'And you,' Jourdan said, suddenly stern, 'did you give any thought to the feelings of those you left behind, Danielle? Zanaide was frantic, and so was the boy who saddled the mare for you. I can quite understand how you must have relished the thought of humiliating me, but Zanaide and the boy . . .'

His look hurt more than any amount of contemptuous words, and for a moment Danielle longed to tell him just how wrong he was. There had been no thought of his humiliation in her mind—only her own should he discover how foolishly she had given her heart into his keeping.

'You are exhausted,' he repeated firmly. 'Zanaide is a soft-hearted creature and begged me not to punish you for your folly.' Before Danielle could object to his choice of words, he added suavely, 'Besides, there is no need, is there, Danielle?'

It was all she could do to simply shake her head. He was right; the ordeal of finding herself alone and lost in the desert had been punishment enough, and one whose memory would live in her mind as long as her love lived in her heart.

'You cannot ride back to the castle tonight,' Jourdan announced abruptly. 'We shall remain here at the oasis and our absence will serve a two-fold purpose. It will give both you and Zara a chance to recover your strength and allow my servants to believe that I have chastised you as they believe a man should chastise his woman.' When Danielle looked blank he added sardonically, 'Surely you have heard the saying, *mignonne*, "A woman, a donkey and a walnut tree, the more you beat them the better they be."' When Danielle recoiled he laughed harshly. 'Do not worry, I have never yet lifted my hand in anger against a woman, and although no woman has provoked me to it as you do, I could not call myself a man were I to do so now.'

'There are other more painful means of punishment between a man and a woman,' Danielle said beneath her breath, thinking of the bitter-sweet agony of his touch, but he heard her, and grasped her arms, swinging her round so that she could see the anger tautening the bones of his face.

Something in her flinching expression must have reached him, because instead of carrying out the threat implicit in his eyes, Danielle was released, while Jourdan turned to secure the mare.

A thick sleeping bag had been dumped on the sand beneath the palm trees and Danielle focused absently on it while Jourdan was busy.

'Yes, I regret that we shall have to share it.'

His crisp words cut across her muddled thoughts. She hadn't got as far as thinking about the purpose of that single, solitary sleeping bag, but now fear trembled along her nerve ends. How could she endure a night in such close intimacy with Jourdan without betraying her feelings?

'Couldn't we go back to the castle?' she suggested woodenly. 'It's only a few miles. Besides,' she added wildly, seeing his expression, 'I want to have a bath . . . I'm covered in sand and . . .'

'If a bath is all you want, we can provide that for you,' Jourdan said easily, motioning towards the oasis itself. 'There is no need to be afraid, we are quite alone here.'

Didn't he realise that was *why* she was afraid? Danielle thought, moistening dry lips with the tip of her tongue, unaware of the smouldering dark eyes fastening on the defensively provocative gesture.

'It doesn't matter,' she began weakly, but Jourdan wasn't prepared to let the subject drop there.

'What is there to be afraid of?' he taunted. 'Surely you are not so naïve as to think that the merest glimpse of your naked flesh is sufficient to drive me into a frenzy of lust? If so you have a lot to learn about men, *mignonne*. Nothing destroys desire as quickly and easily as an unwilling partner.'

Colour stained Danielle's face as she turned defensively away. There was no need for Jourdan to underwrite the fact that he had made love to her simply to ensure that their marriage could not be set aside—she was already aware of that, just as she was now also aware that merely to look upon his tall, muscled frame was sufficient to set her heart thudding with the desire which made her legs tremble weakly beneath her, and constricted her breathing.

'You will find that the oasis is quite warm,' Jourdan continued dispassionately. 'I myself had intended to swim in it, so I can provide you with a towel.'

Swim! Danielle risked a glance at the hard, athletic body of her husband, swiftly masking her eyes with thick dark lashes as she felt her regard returned. Did he come often to the oasis to swim in its tranquil waters?

'Don't worry,' he mocked her, 'I shall not force my unwanted presence upon you, although in different circumstances there can be nothing more enjoyable than the pleasure of the silken touch of water upon one's skin without the restriction of clothes, followed by the pleasure of making love beneath the stars with only the desert to witness the brief communion of flesh which is the nearest human beings can come to reaching Heaven here on earth.'

Shaken by his words, Danielle stared out over the oasis, brushing the fine grains of sand off her skin with a faint grimace. All at once she longed for the cleansing touch of water against her body. Jourdan had turned away from her and was busy coaxing flames from a small collection of brushwood he must have gathered while waiting for Zara to bring her to the oasis.

As though he read her thoughts, he said curtly, 'It is wiser to wait for you to come to me than to go looking for you. The desert is a vast place, Danielle, and I knew that sooner or later you would grow tired and Zara would bring you here.' He glanced at the fire. 'A little primitive perhaps, but comforting for all that. Even in the desert men need the comforting warmth of fire. When you have had your swim we shall eat the food Zanaide prepared for you and drink the coffee I have brought with me in a thermos flask. As a boy I spent many nights here at the oasis—and in other less comfortable parts of the desert. My uncle, your stepfather, has a wisdom not given to many, and during the holidays I spent away from my expensive English public school I wandered the desert with our tribesmen, learning from them what no amount of schooling could ever teach me. At first I enjoyed it as a boy does enjoy such things, but as I grew older I saw past the freedom of a nomad's life, to the poverty and ever-present danger that underlies it, and as my uncle had planned gained an understanding of our people, for the desert tribesmen are as much a part of Qu'Har as the men grown rich on oil and modern technology—more so, perhaps, for they ask nothing of life but the right to live it. Money, position, possessions—all these are paid for with freedom.'

It was the longest speech he had ever made to her, and Danielle wondered if he ever envied the tribesmen their wandering life free from the responsibilities which she now saw were his.

Listening to Zanaide, she had learned much she
had not known before. Without Jourdan to guide
the country and spend its wealth wisely it would
be torn apart on the rocks of greed and jealousy,
and she no longer wondered that he had forced
her into marriage; only that she herself had been
so blind to the necessity for him to do so. Perhaps
if she were to tell him how she felt he would set
her free, for he was not a deliberately cruel man;
she was sure of that now, and when she explained
to her stepfather she was sure that he too would
see the need for their marriage to be set aside,
without any blame attaching to Jourdan. Maybe
tomorrow she might find the courage from somewhere to approach him, but tonight she was too
tired, too agonisingly aware of every masculine
detail of him and her own yearning longing to be
taken, possessed and held by him and never, ever
set free.

With a faint sigh Danielle acknowledged the
folly of her thoughts. She paused twice on her
way to the oasis, but Jourdan was still busy with
his fire and never turned round. Her clothes,
when she removed them, were full of sand, and
she shook it out as best she could before removing
her briefs and running quickly into the water.

It was as warm as Jourdan had promised, and
Danielle luxuriated in the soft caress of it against
her skin, turning over to float blissfully on her
back and watch the stars so far above her in the
midnight sky.

Tomorrow she would be forced to face up to
Jourdan's lack of love for her, but for tonight
surely there would be no harm in pretending a
little . . . The first time she felt the faint brush-

ing against her shoulder she thought it actually was Jourdan, who despite what he had said, had come to join her, but when she turned over languorously, there was no one there, but the soft brushing sensation continued, this time on her legs and thighs. Her skin crawled with icy fear, her scream splitting the silence of the night. By the time Jourdan reached her she was beginning to panic, because no matter in which direction she swam, the thing, whatever it was, continued to brush nauseatingly against her flesh.

Even when Jourdan reached her, grasping her flailing arms, she was so panic-stricken that it was several seconds before she could tell him what had happened.

'Lie still and float,' he commanded her, treading water, while he ran his hands dispassionately over her body. Danielle felt something move and bit back another scream,

'Don't worry. It is a piece of weed, that is all,' Jourdan told her, showing her the trailing greenery. 'It must have become entwined with you when you were swimming.'

A feeling of chagrin overwhelmed Danielle. All that fuss simply because of a piece of weed!

'I'm sorry——' she began in a constricted voice, trying to struggle away from Jourdan's supporting arm, but to her surprise he didn't let her go, instead turning her over so that she was lying above him in the water, his body virtually motionless as he supported them both.

'Are you?' he demanded huskily. 'Perhaps after all this marriage is the Will of Allah, and not merely a result of my own manipulating, for it cannot be denied that He loses no opportunity to make me aware of the perfection of your body, and never more so, *mignonne*, than now when it is enticingly wrapped in moonlit water, and I can feel it trembling against mine, just as you must be aware of my response to you.'

Danielle was, and it was that that made her tremble, her body suddenly wantonly pliant, moulding itself against the hard contours of Jourdan's, her soft sigh lost as his arms closed round her and his lips parted hers in a kiss of lazy exploration. Time seemed to stand still. Danielle wasn't aware of them moving, only of Jourdan. The sensation of sand beneath her feet came as a brief shock, but Jourdan was already lifting her in his arms and carrying her over to the fire which still burned warmly. Droplets of water clung to his skin, and as he lowered her to the ground Danielle unashamedly let her eyes linger on the sculptured lines of his body, her breath catching in mingled awe and emotion. The mingling of East and West had produced a man who surely must come as closely as any human being could to the perfection of Ancient Greek sculpture. Broad shoulders tapered to a lean waist and flat stomach, moisture clung in droplets to the dark body hair which arrowed downwards. Tautly male thighs brushed powerfully against her own skin as Jourdan set her down, not totally releasing her. Her own fingers clung to him, and as though the spell which enveloped her also extended to him, Danielle felt the tension emanating from Jourdan, and heard the harshly indrawn breath he gave before sliding her sensually down the length of his body until her toes touched the sand, his arms tightening as his head bent and his lips began a slow exploration of her face, starting where tendrils of damp hair clung to her temples and tracing the lines of her bones, until her eyes were pleading mutely for him to possess the softly parted sweetness of her mouth and obliterate the last shreds of common sense which urged her to turn her back on him and what could only at best be a few bitter-sweet hours of happiness.

As though the touch of Jourdan's lips swept away the last remnants of her reserve, Danielle felt herself responding to him with a passionate abandon that seemed to find an echo deep within him. He muttered something urgently to her in French as he lowered her to the ground, the heat of his body scorching her as he closed the thick quilted sleeping bag around them both before transferring his hands to her body, and Danielle melted into mindless pleasure beneath his skilled touch.

Her feverish moans of pleasure invoked by his touch were echoed in the ragged harshness of Jourdan's breathing. His fingers cupped her breasts, savouring their passionate burgeoning beneath them, and Danielle needed no urging to encourage him to bend his dark head to the shadowed cleft between them, her own fingers curling feverishly into the solid muscle of his back as he teased first one and the other erect nipple.

His hoarsely muttered words had little meaning for her, their urgency communicated by his shuddering possession of her breast.

Her own lips made shy forays against his flesh, her fingertips delicately tracing the breadth of his shoulders. Her body, acutely sensitised to everything about him, felt the silky crispness of his body hair as his hands slid down to her waist, moulding her to him, her slender thighs crushed against the undeniable arousal of his own.

Her hands were removed from his chest and turned palm upwards to receive his kiss before he replaced them against his body, his own sensual stroking of hers encouraging her to follow suit and discover with heady enjoyment that even the strongest male could be made weak by the touch of a woman.

His hoarse groan excited her senses; her flesh seemed to yield and melt beneath his foraging lips, and when he parted her thighs and slid between them Danielle welcomed his possession with an urgency that seemed only to incite him to deeper passion. Her gasped cry was crushed as his arms tightened, the dampness of Jourdan's skin tasting of salt against her tongue, and then his mouth was on hers, and she no longer cared that it wasn't gentle and didn't want it to be as her own need rose to meet his. They reached the pinnacle together in an explosion of pleasure which left her trembling weakly in Jourdan's arms while he soothed her with soft kisses and her body melted against him.

'So much passion beneath that repressive cool exterior,' Jourdan murmured against her hair, his finger going to her lips as she started to speak.

'No, don't tell me that you felt nothing and that you hate me, Danielle. We both know you would be lying. Be honest enough to admit to the pleasure our bodies give one another. For all your delicate slenderness, you possess a sensuality I have never known in any other woman.' His hand slid from her shoulder along the relaxed lines of her body to her thigh where it lingered warmly, and Danielle knew without the need for any words that his desire for her had not been sated. Something elemental within her responded to the knowledge, and she moved sensually against him, blocking out the memory of what he had just said to her. Sensual he had called her, and deep down inside the words hurt. Did he honestly think she was the type of woman who could abandon herself to passion simply for passion's sake? Couldn't he guess how she felt about him, or did he, because he himself could be governed by desire alone, think that she too was motivated purely by desire?

She tried to sort out her muddled thoughts, but Jourdan was already drawing her down against him, mutteringly urgently against her hair as he wound his fingers through it and tilted her head backwards. Somehow during their earlier love-making they had worked free of the sleeping bag and now the moonlight silvered the length of Danielle's body, no longer cold but warmed by Jourdan's desire, and her flesh quickened once again as his mouth moved sensuously along the silver path of the moon.

'See what you do to me, *mignonne*,' he groaned minutes later, drawing her against him so that she could feel the fierce tremble of his body. 'Let us forget for tonight why we came together, and remember only the sweetness our bodies find in each other.'

The feel of him; the weakness of her own flesh, the love filling and spilling from her heart, erased the last of Danielle's self-control and with a soft sigh she gave herself up to the sweet abandonment

Jourdan was urging upon her, telling herself that whatever else the future might hold at least she would have this!

CHAPTER TEN

WHEN Danielle woke up she was held fast in Jourdan's arms. His eyes opened before she could move away and for a moment she felt sure he must read the truth in hers and know that she loved him.

'Last night was the true beginning of our marriage,' he told her in a husky voice. 'There will be no more running away, *chérie*.'

In her heart of hearts Danielle acknowledged that she no longer wanted to run. Jourdan was her husband and desired her and she would have to learn to be content with that. It was more than many women had.

'Come, we must return to the castle before my people come looking for us and discover the manner in which I punish my errant bride. I fear if I did so they would no longer consider me a fit person to lead them, and would blame your beauty for robbing me of my former strength. And they would not be far wrong.'

Before Danielle could make any response to this he was gone, striding away in the direction of the oasis the sun glinting on his bronze flesh.

He returned half an hour later and crouched down beside Danielle, who was still lying in the sleeping bag, the nearest thing she had seen to a grin transforming his features into a much more boyish mould.

'Up you get, woman,' he told her firmly. 'Lying

there like that you make far too tempting a sight; unless of course you want me to rejoin you?' he added quizzically.

Her heart beating fast, Danielle wriggled obediently out of the quilted bag, wondering what his reaction would have been had she merely remained where she was. A shiver of mingled pain and delight quivered through her at the memory of the lovemaking they had shared, but Jourdan already had his back to her, busy clearing away the previous night's fire.

'When Danielle returned from the oasis he poured her a cup of still hot coffee from the flask he had brought with him, and they drank silently in companionable silence, the tensions Danielle had experienced since her marriage melting away as she basked in the heat of the early morning sun and the pleasure of her husband's company.

All too soon the brief interlude was over. Jourdan rose and walked across to where the horses were tethered. Danielle heard them greet him with pleased whickers, and acknowledged that even as he was the pivot around which life at the castle ebbed and flowed, so he was the pivot of her existence too.

The ride back to the castle was a leisurely one, with Jourdan pointing out various landmarks and showing Danielle the old trade route once used by the silk caravans between China and Persia. He was a knowledgeable and entertaining teacher and Danielle listened avidly, reluctant for their precious time together to end. The hostility which had previously existed between them seemed to have been consumed in the heat of their mutual passion, and if the companionship they were now

sharing was less than her aching heart yearned
for, it was infinitely preferable to anger and indif-
ference.

As they drew closer to the castle Danielle felt
her fragile happiness evaporate. Jourdan was a
man with many heavy responsibilities and she as
the wife of a prominent Arab male would be
expected to take a back seat in his life. For a brief
moment Danielle wished she could hold back
time; that they would always be as they were this
morning; that there need never be duty or responsibilities to come between them. She was being
childish, she acknowledged, when Zara, sensing
her reluctance, slowed her pace, and Jourdan was
forced to stop and wait for them to catch up with
him.

Both stallion and master showed consideration
for their womenfolk, Danielle acknowledged, for
without doubt without Zara and herself to hinder
them, they would be racing freely across the
sand.

The castle cast long shadows over the desert;
her heart held fast in the grip of heavy misery
Danielle blinked away weak tears. Last night for
the first time she had slept in her husband's arms;
once his hectic life stretched out to engulf him
would all she see of him be the occasional visit to
her room and bed when he remembered her
existence.

Danielle's gloomy train of thought continued
as they neared the castle. Someone had obviously
been watching for them, because the massive
double gates swung open at their approach. In
the outer courtyard Danielle saw a dust streaked
Land Rover. Jourdan's frown seemed to reinforce

her own despairing thoughts. The magic they had
experienced together in the desert was not strong
enough to bridge the gulfs between them.
Determined not to let him see the pain in her
eyes, Danielle rode into the courtyard with a false
smile pinned to her face and an ache in her heart.
She saw Zanaide rushing towards her, and felt a
pang of guilt for causing the little maid concern,
then Zanaide was temporarily forgotten as male
arms reached up and swung her down from the
saddle, and she heard Philippe Sancerre's familiar
but unexpected voice murmuring huskily,

'Danielle, *petite*, what is all this I hear about
marriage to Jourdan? Surely you cannot have been
so foolish, little one? If it was a husband you
wanted surely you could have waited for me?'

While Danielle was still trying to gather her
scattered thoughts Philippe kissed her firmly on
the lips, devilment dancing in his eyes as Jourdan
came towards them, his eyes cold.

'The privilege of an old friend, *mon ami*,' he
told Jourdan gaily, 'and one I am sure you would
not begrudge me. Not when you have stolen such
a jewel from beneath my very nose!'

The words were said lightly enough, but
Danielle sensed that beneath them, Philippe was
deeply resentful of Jourdan. Jourdan himself was
looking at her with a cold reproof which made
her long to be back in the desert with him.
Philippe meant nothing to her, she wanted to cry.
He was the only man with the power to hold her
heart, but Jourdan was already turning away, and
Philippe was gripping her arm too tightly for her
to follow him.

After murmuring some instructions to his comptroller, Jourdan turned back to Philippe, his face still cold.

'To what do we owe the honour of this visit, Philippe?' he asked him sardonically. 'I seem to remember that you are no lover of the desert.'

'Of the desert, no,' Philippe agreed, adding outrageously, 'But of your beautiful wife . . . that is a different matter.'

Danielle's cheeks were scarlet. She glanced quickly at Jourdan, wondering how he was taking Philippe's broad hint that they had been lovers. His face was shuttered, his expression inscrutable.

'However, it was not my wish to come to Qu'Har,' Philippe went on. 'It was Catherine who mooted the suggestion. She seemed to believe that you would not be exactly averse to her presence. Of course, then, we knew nothing of your marriage,' he added, glancing at Danielle. 'A sudden decision, I take it, *ma petite*? Or was it merely easier after all to give in to parental pressure? Your stepfather can be a very persuasive man, I know. You are a very lucky man, Jourdan,' he added, seeming unaware of the thick silence of disapproval emanating from the other man. 'A rich and beautiful wife . . . Your uncle chose well for you.'

Philippe took Danielle's hand in his, the gesture far more intimate than their relationship called for, but he was gripping her fingers too tightly for Danielle to withdraw.

'Poor *petite*,' he murmured in a soft voice which nevertheless could not have failed to reach the ears of the man standing so close. 'Sold into marriage like a slave in the market! Now more than ever I

regret my gentlemanly refusal to accept what you
so generously offered the last time we met.
Perhaps if I had listened more to my feelings and
less to the voice of caution urging me to remember
how much my family owed your stepfather's, I
should now be your husband. Ah, here comes my
sister,' he added before Danielle had time to deny
his appalling insinuations. She dared not look at
Jourdan. She had no idea what he was thinking,
but there could surely be only one interpretation
to be put on Philippe's so carefully calculated
words. No matter how much she might try to
erase them she knew that she would never be able
to convince Jourdan that she had not, as Philippe
had suggested, pleaded with him to be her lover.
Clever Philippe, she thought bitterly. Had he
merely been satisfied with claiming to be her
lover, Jourdan must surely have disbelieved
him—but Philippe, perhaps drawing his own
conclusions from the way they had arrived from
the oasis together, had subtly poisoned Jourdan's
mind against her, by insinuating that before he
came along, she had been more than ready to
accept Philippe as her lover. When he added that
to the way she had responded to *his* lovemaking,
he was bound to think her a sensual wanton, eager
to take physical pleasure wherever she could find
it.

Seared with painful agony, Danielle turned
helplessly towards Jourdan, then fell back, the
colour draining from her face, as she saw the tiny,
dark-haired figure clasped tightly within his arms,
her face raised for the kiss.

'Catherine adores Jourdan,' Philippe said at her
side, 'Indeed, *chérie*, you will not be very popular

in our family when your marriage to Jourdan becomes known. My mother and Catherine had high hopes that she would be the one he would make his wife.'

'Catherine?' Danielle stared across to where the other girl was still entwined with her husband, her lips pouting enticingly, as, oblivious to everyone else, she slid her arms round his neck.

'But surely . . . I thought your mother said that Catherine was not yet ready for marriage . . .' Danielle bit her lip as she remembered exactly what Madame Sancerre had said about her daughter. Surely a girl like that could never adapt to the Arab way of life as Jourdan's wife would have to?

'Not ready for just any marriage,' Philippe agreed, 'but marriage to Jourdan is another matter altogether, is it not *ma chérie*?' His eyes hardened slightly as they took in Danielle's flushed, defensive features. His sister had urged him to bring her to Qu'Har, with the promise that if, as she hoped, her proximity would cause Jourdan to propose to her, Philippe himself would not go unrewarded. As Jourdan's wife she would be in a position to do a great deal for him . . . Philippe was a realist. He had not totally abandoned the notion of marriage to Danielle, but such a marriage must inevitably be for the future, and he needed money now. His gambling debts weighed uncomfortably upon him; Jourdon was supposedly already betrothed to a girl chosen for him by his family, but Catherine could be very persuasive, and neither was she too fussy about the methods she chose to get her own way.

She was a fool if she thought that simply by

inveigling her way into Jourdan's bed she could
persuade him to marry her, Philippe had told her
forthrightly, but Catherine had not been deterred.
Her brother was forgetting that their family was
an old and proud one, she reminded him, and
there were ways and means which could be used
to make Jourdan forcibly aware of his responsibilities, if necessary. She had paused delicately, but no further explanations had been
necessary. Brother and sister understood one another perfectly, and Philippe also knew that their
mother, while not approving of Catherine's
methods, would tacitly ignore them to aid her
daughter to what would, after all, be an extremely
advantageous marriage.

When Philippe had wondered out loud how his
sister would cope with the restrictions of life in
Qu'Har, Catherine had laughed out loud. She had
no intentions of living anywhere of the kind.
Jourdan was after all half French. They would
live in Paris, of course!

Philippe looked across at her now, her red lips
parted invitingly as she gazed up at Jourdan, and
then he transferred his gaze to Danielle's pale
face, correctly interpreting the expression he saw
there. So the silly little fool had fallen headlong
in love with her arrogant husband! So much the
better. People in love were known to make great
sacrifices for the objects of their affections. A plan
was beginning to take shape in his mind. Perhaps
coming to Qu'Har was going to prove even more
beneficial than he had originally thought. He
looked at Jourdan, remembering their shared
schooldays and his own resentment of the other,
his superior in so many fields. How sweet it would

be to wrench from Jourdan the prize he so obviously thought his. It had been Sheikh Hassan himself who had told him of his hopes for Danielle's future. He loved his stepdaughter almost to the point of obsession, and in Danielle Philippe thought he saw not only a means of revenging himself on Jourdan, but also a way of making sure that he never had to want for anything ever again. Danielle's marriage to Jourdan, which at first had seemed to signal the end to all his and his sisters's hopes, could, after all be turned to their mutual advantage.

Smiling, he drew Danielle's hand through his arm and swung her round so that she was facing Jourdan and Catherine.

'Catherine is very much in love with your husband. In fact . . .' he paused and seemed uncertain as to whether he ought to go on, but Danielle's heart was already gripped in a vice of pain so agonising that she could not hurt more, or so she thought, until Philippe taking her silence for encouragement continued apologetically. 'In fact . . . both my parents and myself thought that he returned her feelings, otherwise they would never have permitted her to travel out here. The two of them saw a good deal of one another the last time Jourdan was in Paris. He hadn't actually approached my father, but Catherine at least had no doubts, and when his invitation came to visit him here . . .'

'Jourdan invited you here?' Danielle swung round, her eyes enormous in the pale oval of her face.

Philippe shrugged uncomfortably, and said gently, 'Surely you do not think my sister would make such a journey uninvited?'

Out of the corner of her eye Danielle could see Catherine disentangling herself regretfully from Jourdan's arms. Still holding his hand as though she drew support from the contact, she turned to Danielle, her voice softly apologetic.

'Forgive me,' she said simply. 'It is just that Jourdan and I . . .' She paused as though unable to go on, but in her eyes was the expression Danielle fought so hard to prevent showing in her own. She went cold with shock and fear. Catherine Sancerre was in love with Jourdan and he had invited her here to his home knowing that, and knowing also that he was married to Danielle. Whom he did not love, Danielle reminded herself bitterly. Was Jourdan in love with Catherine?

If so, he must never, never learn of her own feelings. Pinning a false smile to lips which threatened to betray her and tremble, Danielle slid her own fingers through Philippe's arm in an imitation of the possessive manner Catherine was adopting towards Jourdan.

'There's nothing to apologise for,' she said brightly. 'In fact it's lovely to have you both here . . .'

Catherine's trilling laughter broke the silence.

'Oh, Jourdan, how unromantic your wife is!' she exclaimed huskily. 'I confess if I were so newly married to you I would not want another single solitary soul around.'

'Danielle is English, Catherine,' Jourdan said dryly, 'and the English see things differently. However, she seems pleased enough to see your brother.'

His eyes were on the hand Danielle had slid through Philippe's arm as he spoke, but she refused to remove it, lifting her head instead to meet the challenge written on his face.

'You must be careful, *chéri*,' Catherine cooed, 'otherwise Philippe will steal your little wife away from you. However, I have not journeyed all this way to stand out in a dusty courtyard and ruin my complexion. Can we not go inside?'

Belatedly remembering her duties as hostess, Danielle called to Zanaide to show their visitors into the main salon, asking at the same time that the maids arrange for rooms to be prepared.

'I should like to wash before I sit down, if that is possible,' Catherine exclaimed fastidiously. 'I am covered from head to foot in sand, and my poor skin is scratched in a thousand places from it. You wouldn't recognise it, *chéri*,' she said to Jourdan.

Danielle overheard the remark and her cheeks burned, but she made no comment. Her soul writhed in torment. How could she hope to compete for her husband's love with a girl of Catherine's sophistication? No doubt Jourdan had not had to teach *her* how to make love.

'Perhaps Danielle would take you to her room so that you can wash there,' Jourdan suggested, glancing at Danielle in a way that made it impossible for her to refuse his implicit command.

Neither of them spoke as Danielle led the other girl towards her room. Danielle opened the door and stood back to allow Catherine to enter. The French girl's eyes were cold as they swept the room before finally lingering on the double bed, patently unslept in.

'Poor Danielle,' she murmured with false compassion. 'Married to a man who so plainly does not want you. You would have done better to persuade your stepfather to allow you to marry Philippe. He at least cares for you, while Jourdan——' her eyes passed insolently over Danielle's slender frame, 'Jourdan is used to women, *chérie*, not awkward young girls. In aiming for him you aim too high and must only be hurt when you fall, is this not so? Did he tell you nothing of me? Of our plans? When we were in Paris we were so close . . .'

From somewhere Danielle found the courage to retort, 'Many women have thought themselves close to my husband.'

Retaliation was swift and merciless. 'Many women have been his mistress, you mean!' Catherine spat at her. 'But between us it was different. Jourdan knows the importance and prominence of our family. He would never dream of insulting me by offering anything other than marriage. And he would have married me, if your stepfather had not offered him such a tempting carrot. Oh yes, I know all about it,' she told Danielle, not adding that it was Philippe who had mentioned the possibility to her, when explaining why the Sheikh had refused his offer of marriage. Catherine was a practical girl. She would have to marry money, but in Jourdan she would have both wealth and sexual excitement, and she had been carefully enticing him towards marriage for several years, hoping to use his innate sense of responsibility and honour to force him into a situation from which he could not extricate himself without marrying her. The information that

Sheikh Hassan wanted him to marry Danielle had come as a shock. An unknown, docile Arab bride she could cope with, Jourdan was after all half French and must want more from a woman than passive obedience, but Danielle was a different matter. The news that Danielle was already in Qu'Har visiting the Sheikh's family had forced her into taking action. She had hoped to use her own time in Qu'Har to force Jourdan's hand in some way, and the discovery that he was already married to Danielle had come as a shock. Her eyes narrowed as she examined the luxurious room. How could Jourdan have married this stupid doe-eyed creature in preference to herself? She studied Danielle's slender form disparagingly, and looked once more at the large bed.

'Jourdan does not share this room with you.' It was a statement rather than a question, and from somewhere Danielle found the resources to reply casually, 'Not always; sometimes I go to his room.'

Anger flashed in Catherine's pale blue eyes. 'So . . . you have shared his bed, but that is not such a great thing, *petite*,' she taunted. 'Jourdan is a man above all else, and as such will take what is offered when there is nothing better to tempt his palate. And then of course there is the succession to think of.' She looked slyly at Danielle, who was standing rigidly in the middle of the room. 'Oh come,' she pressed, 'surely you aren't naïve enough to think there could be any other reason? My dear!' Her eyebrows rose. 'Jourdan is courted and pursued by some of the most beautiful and desirable women in the world . . .'

'Including yourself?' Danielle asked tightly,

regretting the question the moment it left her lips, but it was too late to recall it and it gave Catherine the opportunity she had been looking for.

'With me, it is slightly different,' she purred. 'Jourdan knows that I would never consent to be his mistress. In marrying me he would be allying himself to one of the foremost families in France—quite a tempting prospect, wouldn't you say, for a man whose mother apparently sprang from the French gutters.'

'And you would be content with that?' Danielle asked, trying to turn Catherine's own weapons against her, but the Frenchwoman was tougher than Danielle. She shrugged and smiled condescendingly.

'Did I say I would have to be? Jourdan loves me, Danielle. I already know that. His invitation to me to join him here is merely confirmation that to love he wishes to add marriage.'

'He is already married to me,' Danielle reminded her.

Catherine smiled coldly.

'A marriage of convenience forced upon him by his stepfather, but once you have borne Jourdan a son to secure the succession, he will divorce you.'

It was said so confidently that Danielle could not find the words to deny it.

'You stare at me,' Catherine continued, pressing home her advantage. 'Surely you knew this? The present Sheikh has sons, it is true, but none of them possess Jourdan's astuteness, and besides, Hassan has the final power of decision as to who will rule Qu'Har. It is only natural that he should choose Jourdan, especially if Jourdan should have a son to follow him; a son whose mother is

Hassan's own stepdaughter.'

It was all so logically convincing that Danielle was only amazed that she had not been able to see it for herself. Of course her stepfather would be delighted if she gave Jourdan a son. The child would be almost doubly his grandchild, and a certain successor to the Sheikhdom. How stupid she had been not to see this for herself! Their marriage was not going to be annulled, Jourdan had told her, but he had not told her the other reason he had made love to her.

The room spun dizzily around her, and she reached sickly for the bed. Even at this moment she might be carrying Jourdan's child. The thought nauseated her. It was her own fault; she could blame no one else. It was she herself who had foolishly tried to deceive herself that their marriage might come to mean something more than a union of necessity. Jourdan had said nothing. He meant to divorce her and put Catherine in her place—once she had given him a son. With a child he could remain certain of her stepfather's support, but Sheikh Hassan would do nothing to deprive his grandson of the Sheikhdom.

'If you had a scrap of pride you would leave Qu'Har at once,' Catherine continued. 'Or are you so much in love with Jourdan that you will cling to any scraps he may throw you? How it must amuse him to know you are so pitifully besotted with him that you stay, even though you know that he touches you only for one purpose! I could never bear a man to make love to me knowing he loved another woman and that all he wanted from me was a child.' She laughed cruelly. 'I told you

you had aimed too high, didn't I, Danielle?' and then she swept out, leaving Danielle alone staring sightlessly ahead of her.

Danielle managed to avoid Jourdan for the rest of the day, but there could be no escape in the evening and she was forced to witness the sight of Catherine flirting with him over dinner, while Philippe gave her sympathetic glances and muttered under his breath that it might have been better had Jourdan and Catherine dined alone, because they plainly had eyes for no one but each other.

After dinner Catherine insisted that they play some tapes she had brought from Paris.

'Remember dancing to this the last time you took me out?' she asked Jourdan as a particularly sensual number filled the room. Philippe and Danielle might simply not have existed, and Danielle would not have been at all surprised to see the two of them disappearing together in the direction of the turret room.

Jourdan had barely spoken a word to her since the Sancerres' arrival, and Danielle felt too heart sick to do more than respond with monosyllables when he did.

He did ask her to dance, but she refused, shaking her head, and turning away so that he would not see the glitter of tears in her eyes. He had just reluctantly relinquished Catherine, and she had no wish to be endured, simply as a duty when he really longed to hold the Frenchwoman in his arms.

His expression tightened when she refused, and she was grateful for Philippe's intervention when he suggested that she show him the courtyard.

They had been outside for half an hour when Philippe suggested that they return. The salon was in darkness, the music stilled. As they stepped inside Philippe reached for the light switch, and Danielle bit back a gasp of pain as light flooded the room illuminating the couple clasped in one another's arms, oblivious to everything but their mutual passion.

Jourdan reacted immediately, releasing Catherine, and Danielle felt endlessly grateful to Philippe when he acted with promptitude, drawing her against him, his voice light as he apologised for their intrusion.

There was comfort in the arm he placed round Danielle's bowed shoulders as he led her from the room. She made no demur when he insisted on escorting her to her door, nor could she find the energy to protest when, outside it, he paused, pushing it open and then taking her completely in his arms, kissed her. She felt nothing; neither pleasure nor revulsion; she was simply drained of the ability to feel anything but the raging pain of knowing that Jourdan loved Catherine.

Philippe lifted his head and muttered something and Danielle opened her eyes just in time to see the tall form of her husband disappearing in the opposite direction.

'Most inopportune,' Philippe murmured. 'Never mind, *petite*. There will be other times.'

A week passed. Danielle saw very little of Jourdan—or Catherine. The two of them were constantly together, riding, hawking, laughing. She grew pale and lost weight, causing Zanaide to

exclaim worriedly over her inertia. Philippe spent
a good deal of time with her and made an unde-
manding companion.

One afternoon when Jourdan had taken
Catherine into the city because she had insisted
that she simply must have a breath of civilisation,
Philippe found Danielle sitting in the courtyard,
staring absently into space.

'You have to get away from here, Danielle,' he
announced abruptly. 'You are destroying
yourself, and to what purpose? You are not blind.
You know how it is between Catherine and
Jourdan.' He took hold of her hand and stroked it
gently. 'I know that you love him, *petite*, but
where is your pride? Can you honestly endure any
more? You are a mere shadow of the girl I once
knew. I haven't heard you laugh once while I have
been here. Leave now, Danielle, before he destroys you completely.'

'How can I?' Danielle asked listlessly. What
Philippe said was quite true, and Catherine's contemptuous words still held the power to hurt.
Where was her pride? Was she just going to stay
here until she conceived Jourdan's child? A child
which its father intended to take away from her
and discard her so that he could marry another?
If she really loved Jourdan surely she would want
his happiness above her own, and she had to
accept that his happiness lay with Catherine. She
might not like the French girl with her pale blue
eyes and cruel tongue, but she was not Jourdan.

'If I could leave I would,' she told Philippe.
'But I can't.'

'If you really want to go I could help you,'
Philippe told her. 'The Land Rover is there. I

could drive you to Qu'Har, or if you prefer across the border into Kuwait where you can fly to England.'

'I haven't any money,' Danielle told him. 'I . . .'

'Don't worry about it. I'll lend you as much as you need. And Danielle . . . don't think I'm doing this for purely altruistic purposes.' Her fingers were raised to his lips. 'One day when the pain of this fades I hope you will turn to me and let me be the sort of husband you deserve.'

'Oh, Philippe, I . . .'

'Don't say anything now,' he told her, frowning suddenly. 'It's just struck me that it might not be a bad idea to let Jourdan think that there is something between the two of us. It would certainly prevent him from coming after you, dragging you back here to provide him with a son.'

It was too much of an effort to protest. Danielle was sure that Jourdan would never believe for one moment that she loved Philippe, but for the sake of her pride she agreed, shuddering at the thought of Jourdan coming after her, to drag her back down to the depths of self-degradation she had experienced since discovering that he loved Catherine. Perhaps she might even be able to reason with her stepfather and convince him that he still ought to give Jourdan control of the oil company. She was sure that this was what he really wanted to do, and she had no desire to rob Jourdan of what was rightfully his.

Having gained her consent, Philippe lost no time in making the arrangements for their departure. Catherine and Jourdan were going riding the following morning, he told her one evening after dinner. That was when they would leave. There was no need for her to bring anything with her. With luck they would be in Kuwait by nightfall. He had plenty of travellers cheques and could draw on his father for extra funds. 'Just think,' he comforted her, 'within forty-eight hours you could be home.'

Home! Danielle bit her lip, turning her head away. Didn't he realise there would be no 'home' for her ever again without Jourdan? *He* was her home; her world. And he loved Catherine.

The morning was just like any other. The sun shone brassily from a perfectly blue sky. Danielle heard the sounds of Catherine and Jourdan departing on their ride as she dressed. She went to her window, her eyes searching greedily for what would be her last sight of Jourdan, and as though sensing her eyes upon him, he glanced up towards her window. Just for a moment she longed to rush downstairs, to throw her arms round him and beg and plead to be allowed to stay, but the impulse was ruthlessly squashed. For Jourdan's sake, if not for her own, she must go.

They set out within half an hour of Catherine's and Jourdan's departure. Danielle paid scant attention to the arrangements Philippe had made. It was all she could do to get herself into the Land Rover. He kissed her lightly as they drove out of the castle. Danielle had left a note for Zanaide thanking the little maid for all she had done for her. For Jourdan she had left nothing. He would make all the explanations that were needed once he had seen her safely on the plane, Philippe told her.

Danielle guessed that scant explanation would

be necessary. Jourdan would surely draw his own conclusions and be grateful for the opportunity of regaining his freedom and marrying the woman he actually loved.

As they were heading for Kuwait they were not taking the road to Qu'Har, Philippe explained to Danielle, but one which led away from it.

When he said this Danielle asked worriedly if that meant that they would have to cross the desert, but Philippe told her there was no cause for concern. He had visited Qu'Har as a boy and was quite at home in the desert. They would reach the border within a couple of hours, he confidently predicted.

Four hours later he was forced to admit that this had been a foolishly optimistic claim. Heat shimmered all around them and Danielle was beginning to feel faintly sick. Although sturdy, the Land Rover possessed no air-conditioning and they were deep in the desert in the hottest part of the day, with no sign of the Kuwaiti border ahead.

'We must have taken the wrong turning at that last fork,' Philippe admitted when Danielle questioned him anxiously. He frowned as he glanced at the petrol gauge and muttered, 'We'll have to turn back.'

'Wouldn't it be better if we rested for a while?' Danielle suggested timidly. Her head was beginning to throb agonisingly.

'In this heat?' Philippe scoffed. 'How can we? If we don't keep moving the sun will melt the Land Rover around us. God, it's hot!' he complained, not for the first time, a petulant note entering his voice. It struck Danielle that he had been over-confident and was now not as sure of his directions as he was trying to pretend. Neither was he the ideal companion to find oneself with in a crisis. He complained endlessly about their surroundings—the heat, the idiocy of not having the desert tracks properly signposted, and Danielle, her head throbbing, said nothing. Jourdan had already told her how easily these desert roads were obliterated during sandstorms. Philippe was behaving more like a spoiled child than an adult male, but even the knowledge that they were probably in danger of becoming lost in some of the most inhospitable terrain in the world failed to puncture the bubble of misery that insulated her from normal fear.

The sudden cessation of the Land Rover's normal motion to a series of jerky bumps, followed by Philippe' swearing and crashing the vehicle through the gears to a halt, did little to jolt her out of her despair, and when Philippe clambered out of the jeep and returned seconds later, his face grim, to tell her that they had had a puncture, she simply stared at him, not really contemplating the danger they were facing.

'Do you want me to help you change the wheel?' she asked Philippe, unable to understand the reason for the sudden furious contortion of his expression until he said bitterly, 'We don't have a spare.'

It took several seconds to sink it; several seconds during which Danielle had time to contemplate the truth and find herself strangely unfearful of it. If they had no spare tyre there was no way they could go any further in the Land Rover. No one knew where they were, including themselves, and Danielle knew that unless they were found in the next few hours by some miraculous fluke, they would probably both die.

Once she had accepted the truth a strange sort of calm seemed to descend upon her. Philippe was the one who raved and cursed the exigencies of fate, even going as far as to blame her for persuading him to set out for Kuwait. With new adult clarity Danielle saw that Philippe was basically insecure and juvenile in his outlook on life, and must always find someone else to blame for his own shortcomings. Until now Jourdan had been a convenient scapegoat—Jourdan who was everything he himself was not.

Like a mother with a hysterical child, Danielle soothed him as best she could with platitudes which she herself did not for one moment believe. It was impossible to believe that they would be found, and yet Philippe with almost childlike trust allowed her to persuade him that they might. There was water in the Land Rover, although a pitifully small amount, and although the roof kept off the direct heat of the sun, it was nevertheless stifling inside the vehicle. Danielle was beginning to feel painfully sick, but with Philippe alternately pacing up and down outside the Land Rover and cursing profanely with increasing bitterness she felt reluctant to exacerbate the situation by mentioning her illness.

'Well, I'm not staying to die,' Philippe said violently at last. 'Oh, it's all right for you,' he sneered when Danielle said nothing. 'If you can't have Jourdan you might as well be dead—that's what you think, isn't it?' When Danielle said nothing he continued viciously, 'God, what a waste! You and I could have had fun together, Danielle, and had it financed by that stepfather of yours. Well, I'm not leaving you here to die. I can't afford to,' he added cruelly. 'You're my insurance policy, Danielle, and one that's going to pay dividends once we're out of here. I should imagine Hassan will be very grateful to the man who saves his precious stepdaughter's life, shouldn't you?'

It was in vain for Danielle to protest that it would surely be better to remain where they were, or to point out that the Land Rover made a far more visible landmark than they would. Philippe insisted, and so reluctantly, Danielle followed him out into the burning heat of the desert.

CHAPTER ELEVEN

SHE couldn't go on, Danielle thought wearily. She had no idea how far they had walked, or for how long. It felt like forever. She had protested once or twice at first that she had no hat and that they would be much wiser to remain with the Land Rover, but Philippe had bitterly opposed her objections. She stumbled and fell in the sand, her ankle wrenching awkwardly beneath her. In front of her she could see Philippe. He turned and glowered at her, coming back to yank her painfully upwards.

'For God's sake try to keep up with me, can't you?' he demanded.

Danielle knew better than to ask him where he thought they were going. They seemed to have been following this sandy track for a lifetime. Unlike her, Philippe was dark-skinned and used to the sun. Her face felt as though it were on fire, her head throbbing agonisingly with every step. Their water had all gone hours ago. She thought longing of the cool waters of the oasis; of English rain, and Philippe's outline shimmered before her tired eyes and she felt herself slip into a world filled with hallucinations and mirages.

In one of them she thought she was lying on a soft bed, and that Jourdan was walking toward her. Only it wasn't Jourdan, it was Philippe, his face contorted with anger as he shook her brutally and demanded that she get to her feet.

'All right then, damn you, lie there!' he screamed bitterly. 'I'd be better off without you anyway!'

Danielle was glad when he had gone and she no longer had to listen to his hectoring voice. It was quite pleasant lying here really, or it would have been if her head didn't ache quite so much and her skin feel so sore.

She was having a dream. She was on the beach, lying in the sun, and in the distance she could hear waves, only the waves kept on getting louder and louder and a sudden spurt of wind stirred the sand until it blew in her eyes and blinded her.

Philippe must have returned, because she could hear him speaking, his voice raised in sharp protest while someone else spoke in curt deeper tones in a voice whose icy disdain made Danielle flinch instinctively.

'Danielle, Danielle, can you hear me?'

She moaned and turned away from the deep voice, not wanting to be bothered. Some instinct told her that to respond to that voice would be to open the door to pain, and she had endured enough of that.

'No, it's all right, I'll carry her,' she heard the same deep voice continue. 'She's been badly burned . . . I could kill Sancerre for this!'

There was a sensation of movement, and of warmth which had nothing to do with the fierce heat of the sun. She struggled instinctively against the treacherous lassitude of her own body, sensing a danger far greater than that represented by the harsh strength of the sun.

'It's all right, *mignonne*.' the same deep voice reassured her. 'I know how you feel, but all that matters right now is getting you back to the castle.'

Mignonne. The floodgates of her memory opened wide at the word and Danielle opened her painfully swollen eyelids to stare upwards into the face of the man who was carrying her.

He seemed to have changed since she last saw him; his features had become more drawn, accentuating the arrogance of his profile—and no wonder, Danielle acknowledged, trembling. How galling it must have been for him to learn that far from being free of her, he was obliged to rescue her once again from the consequences of her own folly.

'Don't try to speak,' he told her curtly. 'Your skin is badly burned, and we must get you back to the castle as soon as possible. What on earth ...' He stopped, obviously clamping down on the words, and sensing his question Danielle murmured painfully.

'It seemed the best thing. I just wanted to spare us both further pain.' There was no point now in pretending. He had said that he knew how she felt, and she could no longer keep up the pretence of concealing it. Not having to do so was a tangible relief, and she refused to think further than the moment. He was here; she was in his arms.

His face looked bitterly grim. 'And you thought this was the way to do it? By choosing certain death?

'Philippe thought he knew the way. Everything would have been all right if we hadn't had the puncture,' Danielle protested, moved to defend Philippe. She intended to say nothing about how Philippe had abandoned her—for now, with re-

turning recognition, she realised that that was
exactly what he had done, but Jourdan tossed her
words contemptuously aside, his face an angry
mask.

'Oh yes, Sancerre is a great one for "thinking,"'
he agreed sardonically. 'I've no doubt he also has
a thousand plausible excuses for leaving you to
die.'

'He didn't mean to,' Danielle started to protest, but Jourdan's expression forestalled her.

In front of them was a helicopter which she
now realised was responsible for the noisy 'waves'
she had thought she had heard. Jourdan lifted her
into it, positioning her comfortably on his lap.

'What about Philippe?' She started to object as
they became airborne, but her protests were
waived aside with a curt, 'He will remain with my
comptroller and the Land Rover. When the
puncture is mended they will travel on to Kuwait
as Sancerre first intended.' His mouth a forbidding line, he added bitingly, 'Not even for your
sake will I permit him to enter my house again. I
have had my fill of uninvited guests!'

Their return to the castle was a subdued one.
It was dark when the helicopter put down, and
Danielle learned from the few words that Jourdan
exchanged with the pilot that the aircraft belonged
to the oil company and that he had commandeered
it immediately he learned of her and Philippe's
disappearance.

Ignoring the protests of his household, Jourdan
carried Danielle not to her own room, but up to
the room at the top of the turret, where Zanaide,
who had been clinging anxiously at his side, was
dismissed with a swift instruction in Arabic.

'Your skin is badly burned,' Jourdan told her curtly. 'The pilot of the helicopter has gone to fetch a doctor to look at it. Until he comes Zanaide will sit with you.'

Danielle must have made a small inarticulate protest, because he paused for a moment at the door, turning to study her gravely.

'You wanted something?'

'Only you,' Danielle longed to say, but instead she shook her head, a solitary tear coursing down her hectically flushed cheek.

'Danielle, I . . .' What he had been about to say was lost as the door was thrust open and Catherine stood there, a picture of elegance in the very latest Parisian fashion.

'Jourdan, where's Philippe?' she demanded imperiously, barely sparing Danielle a glance.

'Your brother is on his way to Kuwait.' Jourdan said tersely, 'with two of my men to speed him on his way.'

Catherine flashed Danielle a look of bitter dislike before laughing acidly and coming into the room to place possessive fingers on his arm.

'Darling, was that really necessary?' she purred. 'Poor Philippe, I'm sure he wasn't the only one to blame. It takes two, you know . . .'

'It is not for running away with my wife that I refuse to have your brother beneath my roof for another night, Catherine,' Jourdan replied curtly, 'but because he callously left her to die.'

'Oh, come, darling,' Catherine protested, darting Danielle another venomous look. 'Are you sure you've got your facts right? Couldn't it have been Danielle who refused to go with him? After all, in giving up her position as your wife, she

would be taking a considerable risk ... You
are after all a very wealthy man, while poor
Philippe ...'

It wasn't like that at all, Danielle wanted to
protest. The only reason she had consented to go
with Philippe in the first place was to give Jourdan
his freedom, but a terrible weariness seemed to
be pressing down upon her. Her skin hurt and
her whole body cried out for sleep.

'We shall continue this discussion on another
occasion,' she heard Jourdan telling Catherine, no
doubt wanting privacy to confirm to her that the
fact that he had rescued Danielle from the desert
made no difference to his love for the French girl.

The doctor came and made his examination
with gentle hands. Her skin, being so fair, had
burned quite badly he told her, but it looked
worse than it actually was. Some deliciously cooling lotion was applied to her face and arms, immediately removing most of the pain. It was
something new, the doctor told her in response to
her hazy questions, containing an anaesthetic to
effectively relieve the pain. Zanaide was to repeat
the application whenever necessary, and in addition he would give her a sleeping pill to ensure
that she got some rest. She was a very lucky girl,
he continued, and only Jourdan's prompt action
had saved her from dehydration and ultimately
death.

Danielle thanked him for his care and obediently drank the bitter-tasting liquid he produced.
Whatever he had put in it quickly induced sleep
and her eyes were closing even as he left the
room.

When she opened them again the room was in

darkness, and for a moment she panicked, not knowing where she was or why. A figure moved at the foot of the bed and she cried out in alarm.

'No, it is not Philippe,' she was told in harshly controlled tones. 'By now Sancerre should be on his way to Paris, and if you find my presence here at your bedside unwanted, *mignonne*, try to remember that it is expected by my household. You are my wife . . .'

'A marriage of convenience only,' Danielle cried out bitterly. 'A marriage that . . .'

'You will not talk of this now,' Jourdan silenced her firmly. 'When you are recovered, then we will talk of our marriage and of the future.'

Danielle longed for the will power to tell him that she did not need his presence at her bedside and that he was free to go to Catherine, but it was all too fatally easily to give in to the desire to have him stay. She drew comfort from the knowledge of his presence and the false sense of intimacy it created. Tonight was hers, and she would guard its memory jealously.

It was three days before she was pronounced well enough to leave her bed, and then only to go as far as the inner courtyard, when the sun had lost most of its power. Zanaide had accompanied her, but the maid had gone to bring her a cooling glass of sherbert, and Danielle was alone when she heard the imperious tap of Catherine's high heels on the cobbles. She knew who it was without turning her head or opening her eyes, and she felt Catherine sit down at her side in the seat which Zanaide had just vacated.

'I know you aren't asleep,' Catherine began

without preamble. 'Just how long do you intend
to continue with this farce? Jourdan and I both
know that you are now well enough to leave, but
still you persist in remaining. Why? Do you hope
to persuade Jourdan to continue your marriage
out of pity? Surely even you must be aware by
now that he doesn't want you?'

Painfully weakened by her ordeal, Danielle
could summon no defence. What Catherine said
struck home to her heart. She was well enough to
leave, but she had been putting off the final
decision, dreading taking her final leave of
Jourdan.

'What are you waiting for?' Catherine goaded
her. 'Jourdan to ask you to leave? Have you no
pride?'

Danielle heard the angry swish of silk skirts as
the other girl moved away and Zanaide returned,
but her words remained with her, and Danielle
brooded on them until dawn pearled the sky.
What was she waiting for? Jourdan to return her
love? He knew how she felt, he had told her, and
knowing, undoubtedly pitied her. She bit deeply
into her lip, refusing to cry. Catherine was right:
she did not have any pride. When Zanaide came
in with her breakfast she had made up her mind.
She would leave today, but not as she had done
before. She would tell Jourdan of her decision and
wish him well for the future. Her mind made up,
Danielle asked Zanaide to convey a message to
Jourdan saying that she would like to see him.

All day long she was on tenterhooks, expecting
with every knock on her door that he was going
to enter her room, but it was not until evening,
when Zanaide had dressed her in a breathlessly

fragile silk caftan and led her down to the courtyard, that she saw her husband. He looked tired
and drawn. The strain of all his heavy responsibilities, Danielle thought compassionately,
and no doubt she had added to them.

'Zanaide tells me you want to see me,' he said
as he strode towards her. Danielle was sitting on
the rim of the stone fountain, and found herself
wishing that Jourdan would sit beside her, instead
of towering above her. Now that the moment was
upon her she was finding it incredibly difficult·to
find the words she knew she must. It would be
fatally easy to lapse into self-pity and mutely plead
with Jourdan not to send her away, but for his
sake she must be strong.

'What about?'

This was her cue. Smiling as bravely as she
could, she said lightly, 'About our marriage,
Jourdan. We don't need to pretend to one another—it was a mistake . . .'

In the shadows of the garden his face seemed
to grow taut, a muscle compressing along his lean
jaw.

'I too have been giving our marriage some
thought,' he said emotionlessly. 'I had hoped . . .'
he paused and seemed to hesitate, and then continued smoothly, 'No matter. Our marriage could
perhaps be annulled providing you are prepared
to perjure your soul by saying that we never came
together as man and wife. I should not stand in
your way, it was after all something you never
wanted to happen, and no doubt an annulment
would be more acceptable to the Sancerres.'

Danielle stared up at him through a mist of
pain. Was Jourdan trying to tell her that he

wanted her to lie; to pretend that he had never made love to her? A feeling of bitterness seemed to rise up inside her and choke her. She got to her feet, barely knowing what she was doing, a stiff little voice she barely recognised as her own saying that if he would, make the arrangements she would leave as soon as possible.

She had half expected the French girl to gloat over her at the dinner table, but instead she seemed sullen and preoccupied. The reason became obvious later in the evening when Danielle learned that Catherine was returning to France.

'Don't think just because of this that Jourdan wants you,' she hissed vindictively at Danielle. 'I shall be back.'

No doubt she would, Danielle thought miserably. Jourdan was probably sending her away for her own sake, so that she would not be involved in any way in the annulment of their marriage.

She was back in her own bedroom, and undressed quickly, dismissing Zanaide, who was watching her with pensive eyes. How would Zanaide enjoying looking after Catherine? Danielle wondered. She had grown fond of the Arab girl and would miss her. Her cases were already packed and she had sensed Zanaide's disapproval as she watched her remove her clothes and make the preparations for her departure.

Sleep seemed to elude her, and tonight more than any other night since her marriage Danielle needed its panacea. At last, acknowledging that her overwrought mind was not going to allow her to find oblivion, she climbed out of bed and found the thin silk robe Zanaide had placed at the foot of the bed. In the tower room were the tablets the doctor had given her. One of those would help her to sleep.

The stone stairs felt cold to her bare feet, and too late Danielle acknowledged that she should have worn something on them. The tower door yielded immediately beneath her fingers, the moonlight turning the pale silk of her gown into a cobwebby substance through which the slender lines of her body were immediately visible to the a man seated by the window.

'Jourdan!' Without thinking Danielle released the door, her eyes flying to the divan, where she half expected to see Catherine's seductive form reclining, even though she knew that the French girl had already left the castle. She had thought that Jourdan had gone with her, and if the truth were known, it was this which had contributed to her own inability to sleep.

Jourdan stood up, his own robe doing little to conceal the potent masculinity of the body beneath it, the deep vee exposing the hair-darkened breadth of his chest, making Danielle's heart lurch betrayingly, as she dragged her eyes away from his tall frame. He had been looking at something which he placed face downwards on the seat beside him, before crossing the room.

'I couldn't sleep.' Danielle explained weakly. 'My sleeping pills were up here.' Jourdan was standing so close to her that she could feel the heat emanating from his body. Her legs suddenly refused to support her and she stumbled towards the seat he had just vacated, dislodging a framed photograph as she did so.

Her shocked gasp mingled with Jourdan's

curse, and she reached instinctively towards the floor to retrieve the frame. A shaft of moonlight illuminated the photograph within it, and Danielle stared at it, unable to look away.

'So now you know,' Jourdan said harshly, taking it from her. 'I was in Qu'Har when I learned of my uncle's marriage to your mother. I went to England to try to dissuade him from such a foolish step and instead of doing so, fell head-long in love with a child . . .' His mouth twisted bitterly, pain scored deep in the grooves running from nose to mouth.

'I don't understand,' Danielle whispered. 'That photograph—it was of me . . . I remember having it taken. My stepfather . . .'

'Commissioned it at my request,' Jourdan said harshly. 'You were fifteen at the time, growing from adolescence towards womanhood. I told myself I was losing my mind, but it made no dif-ference . . . I couldn't get you out of it, and Hassan, of course, did little to discourage me.'

'What . . . what . . . what are you saying?' Danielle demanded tremulously, gasping as Jourdan turned suddenly, his fingers grasping her arms as he dragged her to her feet, his face a mask of pain and self-contempt as he said hoarsely.

'Damn you, Danielle, what are you trying to put me through? You know how I feel about you. I didn't want you to . . . I wanted to wait . . . I wanted to give you time to get used to me, to come to feel something for me, but Sancerre forced my hand. He knew how I felt all right . . .'

'Philippe? But . . .'

'You love him, I know,' Jourdan said grimly, 'and if you knew how close I've come to killing him because of it! Jealousy is a very powerful emotion—just as love is a very strong one. God knows I've tried to smother my love for you. You were fourteen, for God's sake, and I was already a man, but I wanted you . . . It was as though I knew what you were going to be, and wanted the woman I could see growing inside the child. Hassan understood, encouraged me even. He loves you and thought it would be an excellent way of securing your future and Qu'Har's, and I didn't discourage him. I wanted you too much.

'I told myself that once you were married to me I could woo you, teach you to love me in return, and then Hassan told me that you had refused to even consider marriage to me; that you wanted Sancerre. I think I must have gone a little mad. When I discovered from Hassan that you were in Qu'Har, I left Paris immediately. The Sheikha knew how I felt; she helped me . . . I wanted you, Danielle, and like a blind fool thought that I could teach you to want me in return. Instead I've stolen from you the right to bestow your love where you wished. I can't say I approve of your choice . . .'

'Can't you?' A deliciously heady sense of excitement engulfed Danielle. She was sure she must be dreaming. This couldn't be Jourdan admitting that he loved her; had loved her from childhood. This couldn't be Jourdan looking so haggard and drawn; so much the supplicant instead of the arrogant, lordly creature she knew.

'Don't play games with me,' he told her roughly. 'Oh, I don't blame you for wanting your revenge . . . Catherine told me you would; told me about how you and Philippe had planned to run away . . .'

How clever Philippe and his sister had been, Danielle reflected, twisting and turning the facts until both she and Jourdan were convinced that their lies represented the truth.

'Catherine told me that you wanted to marry *her*,' she said lightly, still not wholly convinced that she wasn't dreaming.

Jourdan made an arrogantly disdainful gesture, his face hardening. 'Never,' he said succinctly, moving away abruptly. 'Now where are your sleeping pills? The midnight hour is not a good one to share confidences, Danielle, because inevitably, when emotions ride high it leads to the sharing of other things . . . things which are often regretted in the sober light of day, and while I hope I am not an animal governed by basic instincts, neither am I a saint.'

'And you really love me?' Danielle queried in a low voice.

'Yes, damn you!' Jourdan ground out, in a decidedly unlover-like voice. 'Now get the hell out of here before I forget all my good resolutions and take you to bed with me!'

He had his back to her, but Danielle made no move to leave, nor to pick up the bottle of sleeping pills he had placed on the window, and she could almost feel the tension stiffening his body as he waited for her to go.

'Danielle.' It was more of a groan than a command, and it took all her courage to meet the look in his eyes. 'This is your last warning,' he said thickly. 'Go now, or face the consequences.'

When she still didn't move he gave a muttered curse and reached for her, his voice raw with a

longing which was like a match to her own desire.
'So be it,' he groaned, his arms closing round her.
'But why? As a punishment? Or is it just that that
tender heart of yours wants to leave me at least
one sweet memory?'

He was lifting her off her feet, carrying her to
the divan, his fingers trembling over the fastening
of her robe which was discarded with an impatient
haste, baring her body to the hunger of his gaze.

'Aren't you going to kiss me?' she asked in-
nocently.

A hectic flush lay along his high cheekbones,
his eyes glittering beneath the thick lashes. His
body seemed to burn against hers as he flung off
his own robe.

'Danielle.'

It was the hoarse plea of a man who knows he
has reached the limit of his endurance and prays
that he will not be pushed past it, and Danielle
felt his agony as though it were her own, her
control breaking as she reached up towards him,
her arms urging him impatiently downwards,
her body yielding to the fierce heat of his
touch.

'Love me, Jourdan,' she whispered against the
lips he had clamped shut in a tight line, shivering
against him. 'Please love me the way I love you.'

His control broke like the giving of a dam, his
mouth hotly possessive on hers, forcing from her
a sweet surrender to the passion she could feel
rising up inside him.

Not until every inch of her skin had been sensuously explored and worshipped by his hands
and lips did Jourdan allow her the freedom to
respond in kind, their mutual need to assuage

their longing for one another obliterating everything else.

Jourdan's fierce cry of triumph in the ultimate moment of possession reminded her of the first time they had made love, and her body responded paganly to the need to know complete abandonment and fulfilment.

Later when they were both at peace, Jourdan's dark head resting against her breast, his tongue making lazy forays against her flesh, he said softly, 'You little witch. You enjoyed tormenting me like that, didn't you ... getting me to unburden myself to you ...'

'Only because I couldn't believe it was really true,' Danielle responded indignantly, loving the feel of his crisp dark hair beneath her fingers. 'I thought you loved Catherine. She told me you loved her. You said you knew how I felt, and I thought you meant you knew I loved you and felt sorry for me.'

'When in reality what I meant was that I knew you loved Sancerre, or thought I did,' Jourdan added wryly. 'For two comparatively intelligent people we were very easily duped.'

'Because we were in love,' Danielle said softly, her eyes shining. 'Oh, Jourdan ...'

'Oh, Jourdan what?' he mimicked lazily.

'Nothing. Just—Oh, Jourdan, I'm so glad we discovered the truth before it was too late. Just think if I hadn't come up here tonight looking for my sleeping pills, we would have gone our separate ways and never known ...'

'Maybe, and then maybe not. I doubt if, when it actually came to it, I would have been able to let you go,' Jourdan admitted wryly.

'Daddy will be pleased,' Danielle murmured idly. 'He told me that Philippe was exaggerating your murky past and that I wasn't to pay too much attention to what he was saying.'

'Well, it isn't entirely spotless,' Jourdan admitted, suddenly serious. 'Oh, I've never loved anyone else, but . . .' he grimaced slightly, 'there were times when I thought it might be a good idea if I erased your image from my mind, and that's what I tried to do. But never successfully.'

Danielle was too wise to dig more deeply into the past. What was past was past. Jourdan had been a man when she was still a child.

'Are we going to talk all night?' she asked with exaggerated impatience, her eyes wide and mock innocent.

'Why, what alternative did you have in mind?'

The words were tinged with lazy indulgence, but the gleam in the night-dark eyes was far from lazy, and Danielle's pulses raced in answering acknowledgement as Jourdan lowered his head, his voice cool no longer but husky with emotion as he murmured, 'Praise be to Allah, Danielle, for he has given me that which I most coveted, a jewel I shall forever treasure and keep from envious eyes.'

Her own reply was lost beneath the sweetly fierce passion of his kiss, as he drew her down with him into a whirlpool of emotion where nothing existed save their love.

Harlequin Plus
A VERY PRIVATE WORLD

When Penny Jordan's heroine consented to hide her face behind the *chadrah*, a concealing black veil, she retreated into the secluded world Arab women have inhabited for centuries. For in most Arab countries, to be female has traditionally meant staying in the home—as the exclusive property of, first, father and, later, husband. Women do not venture into public without the modesty of the *chadrah*, which makes them virtually invisible to male eyes. Only in the company of family members or other females do they ever lower the veil.

As Western civilization continues to make inroads into the oil-rich desert nations, this custom has been slowly changing. More and more Islamic women are casting off their veils to walk openly alongside men, attend colleges and even start careers—albeit in traditional female occupations, where contact with men outside the family is limited.

Readers rave about
Harlequin romance fiction...

"I absolutely adore Harlequin romances!
They are fun and relaxing to read, and
each book provides a wonderful escape."
— N.E.,* Pacific Palisades, California

"Harlequin is the best in romantic reading."
— K.G., Philadelphia, Pennsylvania

"Harlequin romances give me a whole new
outlook on life."
— S.P., Mecosta, Michigan

"My praise for the warmth and adventure
your books bring into my life."
— D.F., Hicksville, New York

*Names available on request.

**The bestselling epic saga of the Irish.
An intriguing and passionate story
that spans 400 years.**

FIRST...
The Defiant

Lady Elizabeth Hatton, highborn
Englishwoman, was not above using
her position to get what she wanted
...and more than anything in the
world she wanted Rory
O'Donnell, the fiery Irish rebel.
But it was an alliance that promised
only ruin....

THEN...
The Survivors

Against a turbulent background of
political intrigue and royal
corruption, the determined,
passionate Shanna O'Hara searched
for peace in her beloved
but troubled Ireland. Meanwhile
in England, hot-tempered
Brenna Coke fought against
a loveless marriage....